Matt Damon

Titles in the People in the News series include:

PEOPLE
IN THE NEWS

Matt Damon

by Christina M. Girod

Lucent Books, San Diego, CA

Library of Congress Cataloging-in-Publication Data

Girod, Christina M., 1968–
  Matt Damon / by Christina M. Girod.
    p. cm. — (People in the News)
Includes bibliographical references and index.
  ISBN 1-56006-774-8
  1. Damon, Matt—Juvenile literature. 2. Motion picture actors and actresses—United States—Biography—Juvenile literature. [1. Damon, Matt. 2. Actors and actresses.] I. Title. II. People in the News (San Diego, Calif.)
  PN2287.D255 G57 2001
  791.43'028'092—dc21

00-012620

Copyright © 2001 by Lucent Books, Inc.
P.O. Box 289011
San Diego, CA 92198-9011
Printed in the U.S.A.

Table of Contents

Foreword

FAME AND CELEBRITY are alluring. People are drawn to those who walk in fame's spotlight, whether they are known for great accomplishments or for notorious deeds. The lives of the famous pique public interest and attract attention, perhaps because their experiences seem in some ways so different from, yet in other ways so similar to, our own.

Newspapers, magazines, and television regularly capitalize on this fascination with celebrity by running profiles of famous people. For example, television programs such as *Entertainment Tonight* devote all of their programming to stories about entertainment and entertainers. Magazines such as *People* fill their pages with stories of the private lives of famous people. Even newspapers, newsmagazines, and television news frequently delve into the lives of well-known personalities. Despite the number of articles and programs, few provide more than a superficial glimpse at their subjects.

Lucent's People in the News series offers young readers a deeper look into the lives of today's newsmakers, the influences that have shaped them, and the impact they have had in their fields of endeavor and on other people's lives. The subjects of the series hail from many disciplines and walks of life. They include authors, musicians, athletes, political leaders, entertainers, entrepreneurs, and others who have made a mark on modern life and who, in many cases, will continue to do so for years to come.

These biographies are more than factual chronicles. Each book emphasizes the contributions, accomplishments, or deeds that have brought fame or notoriety to the individual and shows how that person has influenced modern life. Authors portray their subjects in a realistic, unsentimental light. For example, Bill Gates—the cofounder and chief executive officer of the software giant Microsoft—has been instrumental in making personal computers the most vital tool of the modern age. Few dispute his business savvy, his perseverance, or his technical expertise, yet critics say he is ruthless in his dealings with competitors and driven more by his desire to maintain Microsoft's dominance in the computer industry than by an interest in furthering technology.

In these books, young readers will encounter inspiring stories about real people who achieved success despite enormous obstacles. Oprah Winfrey—the most powerful, most watched, and wealthiest woman on television today—spent the first six years of her life in the care of her grandparents while her unwed mother sought work and a better life elsewhere. Her adolescence was colored by promiscuity, pregnancy at age fourteen, rape, and sexual abuse.

Each author documents and supports his or her work with an array of primary and secondary source quotations taken from diaries, letters, speeches, and interviews. All quotes are footnoted to show readers exactly how and where biographers derive their information and provide guidance for further research. The quotations enliven the text by giving readers eyewitness views of the life and accomplishments of each person covered in the People in the News series.

In addition, each book in the series includes photographs, annotated bibliographies, timelines, and comprehensive indexes. For both the casual reader and the student researcher, the People in the News series offers insight into the lives of today's newsmakers—people who shape the way we live, work, and play in the modern age.

Introduction

The Quest for Perfection

IN 1996 MATT Damon's phone was not ringing. Most days, he sat in front of the television, munching on Cheerios, hoping to drown his desperation for work by watching and studying good films. His friend and roommate, Ben Affleck, often came home to find Matt in the midst of a messy, haphazard apartment. Matt, who had recently appeared in the film *Courage Under Fire*, was sinking into a depression over the lack of public and critical attention paid to his role in the film. Although a few entertainment magazines commented on his performance as the drug-addicted medic Ilario, most critics swept Damon behind the shadow of the big stars, Denzel Washington and Meg Ryan. After losing forty pounds for the role of Ilario and turning out what he thought was one of his best performances yet, gaining barely any recognition for his efforts was almost more than he could bear. "I wanted to quit acting after that," [1] Damon later admitted during an interview with Oprah Winfrey.

Just when Damon was considering giving up acting to return to college at Harvard University, the phone finally did ring. It was his agent, sending him out on a last-minute audition for the lead role in *John Grisham's The Rainmaker*. Damon jumped at the chance to work with director Francis Ford Coppola, whom he highly respected and from whom he thought he could learn a great deal about acting. From that point on, everything turned around for Matt Damon.

Securing a role in a major film directed by Coppola gave Damon some much-needed leverage in the film industry. This leverage would become the force that propelled Damon toward the kinds of challenging roles and quality scripts he desired. For years he and Affleck had been attempting to bring a script they had written to the big screen, but as little-known actors without much experience, they had not been able to generate much interest in their project. When they finally got the go-ahead to begin making the film, the script of *Good Will Hunting* attracted big names Gus Van Sant for director and Robin Williams for supporting actor. The making of *Good Will Hunting* turned out to be a monument to Damon's creative talent and dedication to high-quality acting.

Just as audiences were becoming familiar with Damon in *John Grisham's The Rainmaker, Good Will Hunting* hit the theaters, catapulting him into the box office limelight. Critics everywhere were praising both of his performances, and Damon received the critical recognition that he had always craved.

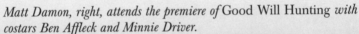

Matt Damon, right, attends the premiere of Good Will Hunting *with costars Ben Affleck and Minnie Driver.*

Damon has had the opportunity to play challenging roles in films, including the lead role in The Talented Mr. Ripley.

Damon's phone is no longer silent. In fact, it is ringing off the hook. Since his success with *Good Will Hunting*, he has been one of the busiest actors in Hollywood, turning out at least two films each year and continuing to work with Affleck writing a new screenplay. More than anything else, Damon is simply thankful that his success allows him to pick and choose satisfying roles in quality films.

Despite his newfound stardom, Damon remains true to his professional and personal principles. Knowing what it is like to be without recognition and respect, he refuses to take success for granted. "Success is not something I've wrapped my brain around," Damon says. "If people go to these movies, then yes, that's big-time success. If not, it's much ado about nothing."[2]

However, Damon has the combination of personality, good looks, and creative talent that Hollywood loves, and rarely finds.

What sets Damon apart from other young actors is his talent, his intense dedication to his film roles, and his ability to bring passion and authenticity to each screen character he portrays. Top it all off with his respect for hard work, and there lies the secret of his potential long-term success.

It took years of practice, striving for perfection, and a decade of disappointment, hard work, and lean times before Damon finally achieved some of the recognition he desired. To understand his success, it is important to look at where he came from: the people and experiences that led Damon to be the person he is today.

Chapter 1

An Influential Childhood

MATTHEW PAIGE DAMON was born on October 8, 1970, in Boston, Massachusetts. The family and community into which he was born greatly influenced his childhood and helped to cultivate his creativity and interest in acting. His parents divorced when he was only two years old and his brother Kyle was five. Damon's father, Kent Damon, worked as a stockbroker and raised funds for low-income housing projects managed by various nonprofit organizations. His mother, Nancy Carlsson-Paige, was a professor of early childhood development at Lesley College. Her liberal views on family life and politics, as well as her role as a working mother, did not mesh well with his father's. "My dad had this *Leave It to Beaver* idea of how life should be," explained Damon, "and it just didn't work out."[3] Nevertheless, Damon's father remained close and active in his sons' lives.

Mother's Influence

Nancy Carlsson-Paige was determined to raise her sons to be imaginative and assertive adults. She allowed Damon and his brother to make as many decisions as possible for themselves as they were growing up. When he was three years old, Damon decided he was ready to give up his pacifier. After he talked it over with his mother, she walked with him to the edge of the driveway and they waited until the garbage truck came. When it pulled up alongside the curb, Damon threw the pacifier in the back of the truck himself. To this day, Damon's mother stands by him on every decision, even if she disagrees with it.

Besides teaching, Damon's mother also wrote books about the influence of television, particularly cartoon characters, and war on children's behavior. She not only deplored television's negative example but believed that children could better spend their time being creative. "So growing up for me was like you'd get some blocks and then you'd have to go make up a game," Damon said. "I was always making up stories and acting out plays; that's just the way I was raised."[4]

Although Damon and his brother were not allowed to watch cartoons, and television viewing in general was limited, the two boys found much to occupy their time. Since creative play was encouraged, the seeds of Damon's storytelling and acting abilities were sown. He had a talent for making up stories, and would tell one to anyone who would listen. In addition, both his mother and father supported his participation in a local children's theater, the Weelock Family Theater, believing it was good for his social development. "My mom and dad thought it was a healthy thing to be in a theater working with other kids," Damon explained. "They thought it was cool."[5] Little did they know how far their son would take this childhood interest.

Superhero Dreams

Damon's theatrical tendencies showed themselves at an early age. "He wore a superhero towel around his neck day in and day out for a couple of years,"[6] said his mother. In fact, when he was just four years old, he wanted to be the superhero Shazam. One day he put his blue cape around his neck and climbed to the top of a jungle gym. With a flying leap he plunged to the ground and broke his ankle.

His theatrical interest began to get serious when Damon was seven years old and went to see the movie *Star Wars*. He later described the impact that movie had on both his and his brother's lives:

We went to see it twenty-five times, [and] couldn't get enough of it. It was this world of total imagination that was suddenly right there in front of us. I was always acting out these parts, and my brother, who went on to become an

Family Cohesiveness

The Damon family is a strong unit that keeps each of its members in balance. Even after the divorce, Damon's parents made decisions about their sons' upbringing together, and major issues were always presented to both parents. His father, Kent, lived nearby in the Boston area and saw Matt and Kyle frequently. He was always around to cheer them on or if they needed someone to talk to. Nancy and Kent remained friends and usually reunited the family for birthdays, holidays, and important events. They even celebrated their "nonanniversaries" as a family. In Chris Nickson's book *Matt Damon: An Unauthorized Biography*, Damon tells of the time the four of them got together to celebrate what would have been his parents' silver wedding anniversary:

> He's [Damon's father] like, "Ah, great. Nuclear family's finally together again." Then the waiter asks if we'd like wine, and Dad goes, "Of course! It's our twenty-fifth anniversary." The waiter announces it to the whole restaurant, and Dad has to say, "Wait, wait! We've been divorced for nineteen years." The whole place just goes silent. Oh, it was good.

Damon is also close to his brother, Kyle, who is three years older. They were sort of "partners in crime" in their creative play as children, with Matt as the actor and Kyle as the costume and set designer. One of Damon's high school teachers, Larry Aaronson, believed that Damon's respect for his brother greatly influenced his decision to go into acting. In Maxine Diamond and Harriet Hemmings's book *Matt Damon: A Biography*, Aaronson says, "Matt's brother was an actor and a dancer and even a comedian in high school. Matty wanted to be like his brother."

Today, his family, especially his mother, is there to support Damon in his newfound success. Sometimes this means making sure his head doesn't get lost in the clouds. This story from *Time* magazine illustrates his mother's perspective on Damon's fame: "When colleagues at Lesley College . . . asked Carlsson-Paige [his mother] for her son's autograph for their daughters, she instead invited the daughters to a discussion group. She showed them pictures of Matt at their age and explained that he was just a regular person, like them."

artist and a sculptor, was always designing these great costumes. It seems we were on predetermined paths from a very early time.[7]

As he got older, Damon began to spend more and more time at the Weelock Family Theater, attending several classes every week. "When I was eight, nine . . . I was [traveling] to Cambridge's Weelock Family Theater, taking classes like pantomime [and] face painting."[8] Although acting was something Damon thought of as simply a fun afterschool activity, it was clearly becoming increasingly important to his identity.

His mother, who viewed Damon's acting as a wonderful creative outlet rather than a future career, reflects on his interest in acting as a small child:

> It's unusual for children to become interested in something really young and then stay with it their whole lives. But that's Matthew. He came to me when he was eight and said, "I know what I want to be when I grow up." And I said, "What's that honey?" knowing exactly what he would say. And when he said, "An actor," I said, "That's nice. Now go out and play."[9]

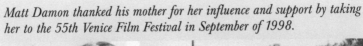

Matt Damon thanked his mother for her influence and support by taking her to the 55th Venice Film Festival in September of 1998.

Damon, however, eventually proved he was committed to acting as he moved into his preteen and teen years and began to seek out more serious opportunities in theater. But at age ten, Damon had no idea that soon his whole world would be uprooted, and he would meet the person who was to cement his dedication to acting.

The Communal House

After his parents' divorce, Damon's mother had moved Matt and Kyle to Newton, a suburb of Boston. By the time Damon was in elementary school, Nancy Carlsson-Paige could see that her son was not happy with the school in Newton. "Matt used to hide under the kitchen table wrapped in a quilt each morning before school,"[10] she recalled. Armed with this knowledge, and wanting her sons to experience a more culturally and economically diverse community, Carlsson-Paige decided to move her family to the more liberal community of Cambridge, Massachusetts, in 1980.

Ironically, soon after the move, Damon expressed a desire to see his old friends again, and his mother, believing he just needed some closure on that part of his life, thought it might be a good idea. "My mother came up with this idea: 'Well, why don't you go back and spend a day there?'" Damon remembers. "But when she called and asked whether her son could return to say goodbye and achieve some closure, the principal said no. I couldn't understand it. The feeling of rejection was so deep."[11] Carlsson-Paige wrote a letter to the principal expressing her disappointment and anger, which Damon carried around with him for a long time before sending it. Amazingly, despite all the rejections his future as an actor held in store for him, this rejection stung him the most, perhaps because he was so young.

In Cambridge, the Damons and five other families purchased a run-down old house on Auburn Street between two Ivy League colleges, Harvard and MIT (Massachusetts Institute of Technology). They agreed to fix up the house by working together, engaging in an "experiment" in communal living, with all six families taking residence in the house. "It was governed by a shared philosophy that housing is a basic human right," said Damon. "Every week there was the three-hour community meeting, and Sundays were

Damon's mother moved the family to Cambridge, Massachusetts, in 1980.

workdays. My mom put little masks on me and my brother, gave us goggles and crowbars, and we [demolished] the walls." [12]

Although in 1980 a communal type of living arrangement would have still reminded people in many parts of the country of hippies, in liberal, intellectual Cambridge it was not such an oddity. At first the ten-year-old Damon felt isolated living among people he did not know, but he later defended the communal living style. "It was a great way to be raised, especially for an actor. Lots of different perspectives, just surrounded by lots of positive human beings," [13] he explained. And although the living room area was shared, each family had their own "apartment."

Most important was the fact that Matt and Kyle were able to attend the more progressive Cambridge Alternative School (which is now called Graham and Parks School). The philosophy at this school closely mirrored the educational and political views of Carlsson-Paige. In addition, the boys would be going to school in a multicultural setting—Cambridge, at the time, had eighty-two different nationalities in its population.

Even though he had moved, Damon continued his classes at the Weelock Theater. Acting, however, remained merely a childhood hobby for him, until he met a kid who lived just a few blocks away who would change the course of Damon's entire future as an actor.

Best Buddy, Ben

Just two blocks from Auburn Street, where Damon lived, was a little boy two years younger than Matt Damon named Ben Affleck. Affleck lived with his younger brother, Casey; his mother, a teacher whose progressive ideas about education and politics were closely aligned with Damon's mother's philosophies; and his father, an aspiring actor and writer who made ends meet working as a bartender, a custodian, and an auto mechanic.

Although there are several versions as to how Matt Damon and Ben Affleck actually met, it seems certain that their mothers' affinity for progressive ideas played a definite role in their spending time together. Of course it helped that the boys had two things they both loved in common–acting and Little League baseball. "We grew up together, and I think we just look at the world in the same way," Damon says about his best friend, who later became his professional writing partner. "He's the funniest guy I know and the best actor I've ever met. Um, I just admire him greatly. You gotta admire a close friend of yours." [14]

At the age of eight, Affleck had already had paid acting jobs, including a regular supporting part in a PBS series called *The Voyage of the Mimi.* This impressed Damon, and prompted him to see acting as much more than the fun classes he took at the Weelock Family Theater. As children, Damon and Affleck spent all their free time together, fueling their mutual passion for acting.

Affleck described those growing-up days: "We played Dungeons & Dragons, video baseball, short stop in Little League, watched Godzilla and Kung Fu double features on Saturdays, [and] followed the adventures of The Super Friends and The X-Men." [15]

Damon Gets Serious

Soon, however, the two friends' mutual interests turned to more mature aspirations. In 1984 Matt Damon started high school at Cambridge Rindge and Latin, an alternative public school, where he finally became involved in more serious acting roles through drama classes and school theater productions. He came under the guidance of drama teacher Gerry Speca. Speca heavily influenced the development of Damon's acting skills, and both Damon and Affleck (who began attending Cambridge Rindge and Latin two years later) credit him with making their careers possible. "Ben and I owe everything to him," [16] Damon has said.

Matt Damon: NBA Star?

Although acting has always been a passion for Matt Damon, as a small boy, he harbored another, very different dream. In grade school he became interested in sports, and for many years spent his summers developing a good pitcher's arm while playing Little League baseball. But Damon's favorite sport was basketball, and he dreamed of one day playing for the NBA. He played for a junior team during the winter months, practicing several hours each day, and he followed the Boston Celtics every season, attending games with his father.

As the years rolled along, Damon never once gave a second thought to the height required to become a professional basketball player (most are way over six feet tall). Finally, when he was twelve, his father sat him down for a hard talk. "I'm the tallest Damon ever to evolve and I'm five eleven. But I'm never going to play in the NBA," he confessed to Damon, according to Chris Nickson in his book *Matt Damon: An Unauthorized Biography*. His father pointed out that his basketball idol "Tiny" Archibald was called tiny because he was one of the shortest athletes in the sport at 6' 1".

At such an impressionable age, seeing his dream fall flat could have crushed Damon. But instead he rethought his plans for the future and decided to pursue another passion—acting. For Damon, the decision was motivated by his desire to be the best at whatever he chose to do in life.

Damon attended an alternative public high school, Cambridge Rindge and Latin. It was here that Damon (left) began to seriously consider a profession in acting.

In high school, Damon's dedication to character development was evident. Early on Damon loved to try out for many different types of roles in many kinds of scripts. During his high school years, Damon played the parts of a priest, a Sandinista rebel, Humpty Dumpty, and the lead in the musical *Guys and Dolls*. He approached his roles with the same great energy he had brought to his classes at the Weelock Theater. Drama teacher Speca remembered this energy when he described Damon's first appearance in a school play, in which he played a samurai in an adaptation of a Kabuki play: "He was this little dervish, running around, rehearsing his part, all of his moves, making sure everything was just right." [17]

With time, Gerry Speca's influence began to rub off on Damon. Much of this was due to Speca's high expectations for his drama students. He not only directed the students in plays but encouraged them to write their own scripts. Speca gave constructive criticism, had the students act out their scripts, and then had them rewrite them. This practice may have honed Damon's writing skills years before he wrote the one-act play in college that later became the film *Good Will Hunting*. "He taught kids self-discipline—how to take responsibility for themselves,"[18] Ben Affleck said of Speca's teaching. The guidance paid off quickly: In his junior year of high school, Damon was part of an acting troupe that won the *Boston Globe* youth drama award.

Speca, however, is not inclined to take all the credit for Damon's success. Early on he saw that the fledgling actor had a lot of drive and a lot of potential. "From the time he was fourteen or fifteen, you could see the incredible presence he had on stage," Speca later said of Damon. "Even with his squeaky voice, he never wasted a move on stage. He knew even then what it took to be a good actor."[19]

Going Professional

By this time, however, Damon was ready for something more challenging than high school theater productions. As he watched Affleck's career continue to rise (he secured a role in the 1984 ABC afterschool special *Wanted: The Perfect Guy*), Damon grew increasingly frustrated by his own lack of professional experience. He attended as many open auditions in the Boston area as he could, but time after time he was rejected.

Then one day, Damon and his friend Affleck auditioned for a television commercial for the clothing chain T. J. Maxx. To Damon's amazement, both of them were chosen to do the commercial. It was Damon's first paid work for acting, and the experience solidified his desire to be a professional actor. Soon after, Damon and Affleck began meeting at lunch to discuss long-range plans for their acting futures. "We used to have what we called 'business lunches' in high school, which meant we met in the smaller cafeteria and got a table—and worked out some business plans," both Damon and Affleck later recalled. "We were really nerdy."[20]

Affleck's younger brother, Casey, however, thought Damon was anything but nerdy. "He was the guy who sat in the back of the bus always making out with his girlfriends,"[21] Casey said of Damon's popularity in high school. Popularity notwithstanding, nothing—not girls, not grades—could stand in the way of Damon's commitment to acting.

Affleck, the veteran by comparison, suggested that Damon audition for his talent agent and try to get signed on. With an agent, Damon thought it would be easy to find paid roles. With this in mind, at the age of sixteen he went to his parents and announced that he intended to act professionally and that to do so he needed an agent.

His parents were very skeptical, especially his mother. "Did I raise you?" Carlsson-Paige exclaimed after his announcement. "That's just an egomaniacal [self-centered] pipe dream. How does it help other people?"[22] His mother, true to her liberal principles, believed Hollywood was nothing more than empty promises that led to a life of excess. Both of his parents were worried that his dream of being an actor would mean a life of rejection and poverty for their son. However, Carlsson-Paige had always allowed her children to make their own decisions. Reluctantly, they told Damon that he could go to New York City for the audition with Affleck's talent agent as long as he paid for the trip himself. Accompanied by Affleck, Damon used the $200 he had earned from the T. J. Maxx commercial to pay for his train ticket to the talent agency.

The Agent

When they arrived in New York City, the harsh reality began to sink in. The agency was small and drab, and the phones were eerily silent. The office was so quiet that Damon wondered if the agency was actually doing any business. To his surprise, when Affleck announced himself, the agency failed to recognize his name. It was then that Damon learned that Affleck had obtained almost all of his acting jobs by attending open auditions, not from agency referrals.

However, Damon pushed away his doubts, later describing his view of the experience: "We were the two chumpiest kids in the world—Ben's thinking he's the biggest star in the world, and he's going, 'This is Matt, he's an actor, too!' and I'm kinda too cool to talk. And they said, 'Oh, yeah, we'll represent Matt too.'"[23]

Growing up, Damon's best friend, Ben Affleck, shared his dream of acting.

Damon naively thought that in just a few weeks he would be getting phone calls from the agency for auditions in television and movies—he was certain his career would catch up to Affleck's now. But it did not. In fact, he never once heard from that agency. However, at the time, simply believing he had someone looking out for his professional interests gave him the confidence to keep his dream alive.

This belief also allowed Damon to settle down and concentrate on his schoolwork. Although he had always been an excellent student, maintaining high grades these last two years was important because soon it would be time to apply to college.

"Mom, Do You Want My Green Stuff?"

In the meantime, Damon continued honing his craft under Speca's tutelage and acting in school productions. His first big break came in 1988 when he was cast in a film that starred several other unknowns. The film was *Mystic Pizza,* which catapulted Julia Roberts into the Hollywood spotlight. Damon's part was very small—one line, in fact—but it was in a real motion picture, something that best buddy Ben had never done. Damon played the part of Steamer, the boy who asks his mother during a dinner scene, "Mom, do you want my green stuff?"

Despite the obscurity of the role, the experience of working on a real movie set boosted Damon's confidence. After filming his scene, Damon realized that his passion for acting lay in the art of film. Television and theater were all right, but he felt that the most intense roles were to be found in the movies. Both he and Affleck decided then that they would concentrate on getting film roles above all others. Later in 1988 Damon made good on this promise by appearing as an extra in *The Good Mother*, with Diane Keaton. Regardless of how small the part was, Damon believed that his career was on the rise. Back at Cambridge Rindge and Latin High School, he poured his energy into his studies and waited for his agent to call.

Preparing for College

By the time his senior year rolled around, Damon was ready to start applying for college admission. Much to his surprise (and his

Damon, here a high school senior, applied to Harvard at his mother's encouragement.

mother's gratification), his high school principal encouraged Damon to apply to Harvard. Although his grades had always been good, he had never considered himself on the academic level of Harvard students. He decided to take up his principal's suggestion and apply, but Harvard was not his first choice because it wasn't an acting school. Damon wanted to go to a college that had an outstanding drama program, and the programs at both Columbia University in New York and Yale University in Connecticut were the best in his opinion. In addition to Harvard, he applied to ten other schools.

Part of the reason Damon did not want to attend Harvard was that, since it was a local school, he would continue living at home. He felt he might be missing out on a big part of the college experience by not moving out on his own and to a place he had never been before. But all that changed the day the acceptance letter from Harvard arrived. Damon never considered he would actually be accepted to one of the most difficult schools to get into in the country. The realization was even more amazing in light of the fact that he had openly admitted in his application that "For as long as I can remember, I've wanted to be an actor."[24]

In June 1988 Damon graduated from high school. Throughout the summer he and Affleck continued to plan out their futures, attending auditions and working as extras in anything they could find. But the fall was drawing near, and Harvard was right around the corner. Matt Damon was about to enter a highly intellectual and stimulating environment that would shape his developing acting career in ways he never could have predicted.

Chapter 2

The Harvard Years

As Matt Damon transitioned from high school student to college student, he submerged himself in the diverse student population and literary climate of Harvard University. He would learn many things about human nature that he would eventually use in his acting. Moreover, although the high academic standards Harvard imposed on its students proved a challenge to balance when he was busy acting, they would also help him keep his sanity when acting jobs were scarce or nonexistent.

Entering Harvard

In the fall of 1988 Matt Damon began his freshman year at Harvard as an English major. Although he had gained admission, Damon continued to feel like he was not in the same league as his classmates. "It's interesting because I grew up in Central [Square] and we are proprietary [possessive] about our city—we kind of viewed Harvard students in a different light," Damon explained. "I always had an underdog complex growing up, even on an unconscious level."[25]

Damon was definitely not the "underdog" he thought himself to be, however. Most Harvard students spend hours outside of class studying, including the weekends. Damon, who was attending college on a partial scholarship, not only kept up with his coursework but somehow managed to find time to keep going to auditions and acting with a few local theater groups. In addition, he took script-writing and drama classes on the side.

In retrospect it might seem odd that Damon opted to attend a liberal arts college rather than a theater conservatory that would have allowed him to focus all his studies on acting.

Damon, however, believed that a well-rounded education would better prepare him for his chosen profession, as he explained in an interview years later:

> Ben, for instance, is probably the most well-read person I know, and he hasn't even finished college and he's been to a number of them. I think that a liberal arts education is very important—you know, invaluable—because it gives you a basis in a bunch of different things. That's why I made the decision not to go to a conservatory. In the arts, you'll have a huge foundation to draw from and your art is going to be much better because of that.[26]

The Wheeler Effect

During Damon's freshman year, he began taking drama courses taught by professor David Wheeler, a nationally acclaimed drama coach who once helped Al Pacino prepare for his roles. Wheeler's classes not only broadened Damon's acting abilities but showed him just how much he still had to learn to become a true professional. He learned to use more subtle techniques for conveying emotions and ideas in his roles, including shadowing, a way of using facial expressions and body language to represent emotions vaguely.

Although Damon practiced his new skills in college and local productions, he never lost sight of his primary focus—films. He began to cut back on local projects so that he would be available for film roles. "I would have done [more plays] if I could guarantee that I would stay a whole semester," he said. "But a lot of times I wasn't, so they'd say, 'Well, this show is going up in a month,' and if I knew I wasn't leaving that month, I'd do it."[27] Moreover, he finally got himself a real agent, who regularly sent him out on promising auditions. But it was not until his sophomore year that he won his first substantial role.

Rising Son

During his second year at Harvard, Damon auditioned for a role in a cable television movie called *Rising Son*, starring veteran actors Brian Dennehy and Piper Laurie. He beat out fellow fledgling

Cambridge vs. Boston: Two Neighboring Worlds at Odds

Matt Damon spent the first ten years of his life in the upper-middle-class areas of Boston, and even after he left Boston, he spent time at his father's home, which was located in an upscale neighborhood. Growing up he overheard conversations that often revealed social prejudices based on wealth, occupation, race, or gender. He had also seen these attitudes in action, including the controversy over busing in the Roxbury suburb, which erupted in ugly racial confrontations.

Cambridge is almost the opposite of Boston in every way. It is socially diverse, a university town of such prestigious institutions as Harvard, Radcliffe, Lesley College, and the Massachusetts Institute of Technology (MIT), and it has an almost bohemian atmosphere. Damon described the town as being somewhat like a world unto itself when he said, in a quote from Chris Nickson's *Matt Damon: An Unauthorized Biography*, "Cambridge is not that big of a town [about 100,000 residents]. It's like the People's Republic of Cambridge." Living in Cambridge offered Damon a more balanced view of the world, which challenged the prejudices he had observed in Boston. Here he also went to school with students who represented a mix of religions, races, and economic backgrounds.

Years later, Damon would integrate his knowledge of both of these social and political climates into the script that became *Good Will Hunting*. It was his understanding of the social prejudices of wealthy Boston and the unfaltering pride of South Boston that allowed him to create the character of Will Hunting. His experiences in the intellectual circles of Cambridge also allowed him to make the psychologist Sean McGuire a believable character, one who had also been shaped by South Boston in his youth. Both Boston and Cambridge had shaped Damon's philosophy about life. In a *People* Online interview, Damon explained how this was reflected in the story of *Good Will Hunting*: "A lot of things were important to us [Damon and cowriter Ben Affleck] writing this script: just treating people nice, not having regrets in the world, being responsible in your relationships and the way you treat other people. That's our philosophy."

actors Chris O'Donnell and Brendan Fraser for the role of Charlie Robinson, the son of an auto factory foreman (played by Dennehy) who loses his job and then his senses when he learns that Charlie intends to quit medical school. The part was the first professional role with some meat to it, including several highly emotional scenes where Damon's and Dennehy's characters clash.

Despite the excitement of winning his first substantial acting job, Damon worried about the time that he would have to spend away from college. The production schedule called for Damon to be in the studio or on location for just two months, but he would be taking a whole semester off from Harvard, and he knew he would have to work extra hard to catch up when he returned. His mother and some of his teachers were worried that acting was creating a diversion from his studies. But Damon had made it known to everyone—parents, friends, and teachers—from the beginning that becoming a respected actor was his primary goal. Everything else had to come second. Only Ben Affleck, who was feeling an identical pull between school and acting, understood, and constantly supported Damon's efforts and decisions.

On the set of *Rising Son*, however, Damon set aside his worries and immersed himself in the character of the troubled Charlie Robinson. He finally had the chance to use all that he had learned over the past few years and prove himself to critics in the film industry. Although *Rising Son* was only a television film, released in 1990 on TNT (Turner Network Television), the critics did notice Damon and praised his performance. The *New York Times* deemed his acting "right on target," and the *Boston Globe*'s Jack Thomas went so far as to report, "Remember the name Matt Damon. If he doesn't become a movie star, my name is Robert Redford."[28]

For Damon, the opportunity to do *Rising Son* with respected names like Dennehy and Laurie meant the chance for an on-the-job learning experience. He listened to stories they told of sets and fellow movie stars they had worked with in the past, and he watched what they did on and off the set—how they carried themselves, how they added dimension to their characters using subtle hints of emotions through a look, a move, or tone of voice. He stored away all that he learned in his growing repertoire of professional know-how and came away hungry for more.

Back to School

When he finished filming *Rising Son*, Damon returned to Harvard. At first he felt somewhat displaced to be back home and shifting his energies from the movie set to books. Fortunately, he managed to regain his focus on college, although he was now behind most of his classmates. All along, though, Damon seemed to understand the value of staying in college. He intended to graduate, albeit just a little later than everybody else. "I went back to school and I really dug it," Damon said. "Where else can you relax and study Japanese culture…? I realized how great it was to be in school, how it gave me a kind of freedom that I may never have again in my whole life." [29]

He continued to go on auditions that his agent found for him, but for a while nothing materialized. Damon was not concerned, however, still basking in the glow of his television movie experience. In the meantime he felt content to concentrate on his studies, much to his mother's relief. He finished out the spring semester of 1990, and when fall rolled around he was still able to commit himself to school.

At Harvard, Damon majored in English and took script-writing and drama classes on the side.

But Matt Damon could not go months without some sort of acting in his life, and during the fall semester of 1990 he participated in a play produced by Harvard's North Theatre Company. This company was actually the professional branch of the student theater on campus, which gave Damon the opportunity to work with other professional actors while still in school. Although he enjoyed the work, he longed for the big screen. That was where the big names were, and where Damon felt he could learn from the best trade artists in the industry. "The only way to get better was to apprentice yourself to the masters," Damon later commented. "I think the masters of today are in films—people like [Robert] Duvall, Denzel Washington, Mickey Rourke, Jon Voight, Frances McDormand, Terry Kinney, Sam Shepard . . . I feel like I grow exponentially when I watch them."[30]

Indeed, Damon took every spare moment he had to study the masters of acting. He and Affleck, who had graduated high school in 1990 and begun college at the University of Vermont in Burlingame, continually watched movie videos, picked apart every technique, noticed every subtlety, took notes, and practiced what they learned by performing in front of each other. Damon took this practice very seriously and incorporated every bit of it in his performances, as he explained in an interview years later:

> I'm always pleased with my performances because I know that I couldn't do it any better. I always try my hardest, give it all I've got. If people don't like it, then they don't like it, that's totally up to them. But, I'll never have a regret about it. Just do whatever it takes to get to the truth of the character. I don't think there's any length that you should not go to do that. That's what we do for a living.[31]

Equally important, the classes Damon took to fulfill his requirements as an English major were contributing to his writing skills. He drank up the exposure to the great literature of the Western world and relished the intellectual exchange of ideas with classmates, incorporating his understanding of life into his writing. As wonderful as the college life was, however, Damon began to itch for the film set again after nearly a year with no opportunities on the big screen.

School Ties

In the middle of his junior year at Harvard, Damon's agent sent him on an audition for a film that offered a number of promising roles for young ambitious actors with talent. It was a Paramount Studios feature called *School Ties*. The film, set in a 1950s prep school, is about a Jewish student attending on an athletic scholarship who faces intolerance from his rich classmates and undergoes a personal battle to stand up for his beliefs. Damon was cast in the role of Charlie Dillon, an angry student with racist views caught between the expectations of his wealthy and influential family and the realization that he lacks the confidence and the strength of character to stand on his own two feet.

Although *School Ties* was a major film production, it lacked the big names that normally draw publicity to a film and speed along its production. All the roles were filled by young aspiring actors at roughly the same stage in their careers as Damon. He found himself cast alongside not only his friend Ben Affleck but also Brendan Fraser (in the starring role), Chris O'Donnell, and Cole Hauser.

Once again Damon found himself taking a leave of absence from Harvard, since the filming of *School Ties* had been scheduled during the first half of 1991, at the end of his junior year. The production schedule was delayed, however, and Damon, along with many of the other actors cast in the film who had taken time off from college, was forced to wait. Finally, he decided to go ahead and enroll for the spring semester of 1991, figuring he could drop out of his classes and retake them later if the set of *School Ties* suddenly called him. But the semester passed without interruption, as did the summer.

For Damon the wait was excruciating. He was learning the hard way that simply winning a role in a big film was no guarantee he would actually make the movie. Paramount could scrap the entire project at any time. And because he had committed to do the film, he could not audition for other roles in case the production of *School Ties* began. Damon did continue to act in college plays, but again he could do only short-term productions. He was determined to hold out for *School Ties*, convinced that this was the role that would catapult his career forward. He knew the script was good and hoped it would be well received at the box office.

Damon took time off at Harvard to make School Ties. *The cast, clockwise from center: Brendan Fraser, Randall Batinkoff, Andrew Lowery, Anthony Rapp, Chris O'Donnell, Ben Affleck, Cole Hauser, and Matt Damon.*

At last *School Ties* scheduled production to begin in the fall of 1991, and Damon prepared to take off the first semester of his senior year at Harvard. In September he and Affleck traveled to Concord in eastern Massachusetts, where they would be living for several months during the filming of *School Ties.* He felt prepared for his role and eager to get started after spending the previous summer practicing his lines and perfecting the nuances of his character.

For Damon this was the biggest thing he had ever done, the closest he had come to living his dream as a professional film actor. As he had on the set of *Rising Son*, he approached the experience of making *School Ties* as an opportunity not just to do what he loved but to learn more about the film industry and grow as an actor. He soon learned that making a feature film was quite different from making a television movie. Since the budget was larger, *School Ties* was produced at a slower pace, allowing for numerous retakes if the director, Robert Mandel, thought they were needed. By the time the filming was wrapped up, Damon was ready to return to Harvard, anticipating the release of *School Ties* in 1992 and the attention he was sure it would bring to his acting abilities.

Disappointment

Damon, like many of the other young hopefuls who took part in *School Ties*, soon found out that it takes more than a good performance in a good movie to make the phone ring. He had naively believed that *School Ties* would be his ticket to the big league, but even small parts were not forthcoming. To Damon, the fact that no one in Hollywood even noticed his work in *School Ties* seemed unfathomable. He later said, "I thought my performance was pretty good, but I didn't have a publicist; I didn't do many interviews and the phone just didn't ring." [32]

To make matters worse, *School Ties* did not become the box office hit Damon and his costars had hoped for. *Entertainment Weekly* praised the film as being "made with honesty and intelligence . . . [and] puts a human face on racism." [33] On the other hand, it was criticized for not delving deeper into the issue of intolerance, and for having a fairly predictable ending. Although the acting was deemed excellent, the cast was judged as an ensemble, and Damon received no individual praise for his performance as Charlie Dillon.

Disappointed in the failure of *School Ties*, Damon threw himself into his studies back at Harvard. Disheartened, he wondered for the first time if he *would* be the successful actor he had planned and worked so hard to become. College was his only solace and kept him busy and focused through the days ahead. Even Affleck, who had weathered the same dose of disappointment after the release of *School Ties*, was not there to help him keep going.

Ben Affleck had dropped out of the University of Vermont during the filming of *School Ties*, and at the start of 1992 he had packed up and driven out to California. He wanted to be where the center of the film industry was, and since it was in southern California, Ben transferred to a college there, thinking he could more easily pursue acting jobs. Damon, on the other hand, wanted to stick with Harvard, so he stayed put in Cambridge.

A Script Is Born

It was about this time, at the beginning of his senior year, that Damon took a creative writing class taught by Anthony Kubiak, for whom Damon developed a strong admiration. Kubiak assigned his students to write a short story. Damon got excited about the assignment and said, "I handed it in and it didn't really go anywhere, but it had a couple of these characters. [Kubiak] told me I should keep writing it. . . . I kept telling him that I couldn't end it, but he would say it was a full-length [piece] and [that I] should

Damon's role as Charlie Dillon in School Ties, *did not launch his career, but it allowed him a chance to develop his acting skills.*

write it into a full-length piece. So he really encouraged me to do it." [34] Eventually Damon developed the story into a one-act play for a directing class he was taking with David Wheeler. This script was the basis for the screenplay that would one day become *Good Will Hunting.*

Enthralled as he was about developing his own script, it did not compare to the excitement he harbored when his agent sent him to New York right before Christmas in 1992 to audition for a part in a movie starring the highly respected Gene Hackman and one of Damon's personal idols, Robert Duvall. The film was *Geronimo: An American Legend,* and before the new year had started Damon learned he had been cast in the film. At last, Damon thought, he was back on track, and this time he was doing it with the masters.

High Hopes for *Geronimo*

At the beginning of 1993 Matt Damon again told Harvard school authorities he would be taking a leave of absence, since filming for *Geronimo* was set to begin before the end of the spring semester. In May he traveled to the red rocks and desolate valleys of Moab, Utah, to begin preparing for the film production. Besides learning as much as he could from Hackman and Duvall, Damon had to learn other skills essential to this movie—like riding a horse.

Damon was cast as Second Lieutenant Britton Davis, the narrator of the story and one of the main characters in the film. As Davis, Damon plays a young, rather naive officer just out of West Point who is thrust into the 1870s western frontier of America. As the story unfolds, the viewer witnesses his transformation from a cocky army kid to a mature, wiser man who learns the "truth" about the army's treatment of the Native Americans from his first-hand observations during the military's pursuit of Geronimo.

Although he had a lot of screen time, there were no big scenes for Damon's character in the movie. Despite this, he did what he could with the role, fleshing out emotions and ideas mainly through expressions in the eyes. He wanted to take his character beyond what the scene asked for, adding a deeper dimension to the story Lieutenant Davis was telling. Adding subtle emotion was a challenge in a film that was made with an objective, somewhat unemotional approach to one of America's most celebrated and

Damon took another leave of absence from Harvard to play Second Lieutenant Britton Davis in Geronimo: An American Legend.

controversial Native American figures. Columbia Pictures said, "We're not telling the story of the spiritual Sioux. We're telling the story of the Apache; the Spartans, not the Athenians. Their art was war. That's the way things are."[35]

From the beginning, everyone, including Damon, had high hopes for *Geronimo*. Unlike *School Ties, Geronimo* was virtually guaranteed to be made since major stars like Hackman and Duvall were already committed. Moreover, these big names meant big publicity, and long before its release, *Geronimo* was being heralded as a major motion picture. To top it off, the film would be riding on the crest of popularity created by the 1990 box office sensation *Dances with Wolves*, another movie about Native Americans. The public seemed ready and eager for stories that depicted Native Americans in a positive way, rather than the romanticized "brave cowboy and savage Indian" westerns of the 1950s and '60s.

Damon believed that this time, if the movie did as well at the box office as it was expected to, his career would receive the boost it needed. All he needed was public notice and critical recognition, and then scripts would start falling into his lap—or so he thought.

Chapter 3

A Dash of Good Will

Dᴇsᴘɪᴛᴇ Dᴀᴍᴏɴ's ʜɪɢʜ hopes for *Geronimo*, he would soon discover that playing a quality role with well-respected actors did not necessarily lead to critical or commercial success. More than anything, Damon wanted a role that would showcase his talents, but such roles were difficult to obtain. As he plodded along in his fledgling career, he began to see that the only way to get such a role was to create one himself. This time in his life was fraught with obstacles and setbacks, but Damon would not let these things stand in the way of his writing a script with a tailor-made role that would challenge his acting abilities and allow his talents to shine.

Leaving Harvard

During the making of *Geronimo*, Damon took the time to reconsider the direction his life was taking him. He loved Harvard and the intellectual and academic challenge it offered him, but he could not deny that film acting was the central passion of his life, the core of his identity. He was working with the icons of the industry now, and there was no going back to smaller projects. By the time he finished the interior scenes that were shot in Los Angeles, Damon had made a decision. He walked away from Harvard just twelve units short of his bachelor's degree and moved in with Ben Affleck in a small apartment in Eagle Rock, California.

After the filming of *Geronimo* wrapped, Damon knew he was gambling the best education in the country on the stakes that this movie would deliver its promise of success. He figured he would be too busy making movies to continue with college, and though he preferred the East Coast to the West, he did not want to have to continually travel back and forth across the country to work. Back in Cambridge, his mother worried about Damon's future in California, deplored the Hollywood lifestyle, and mourned his lost education.

The *Scent of A Woman* Audition

During the shooting of *School Ties*, Damon got to know his costars, who became known as the "Frat Pack." The members of the so-called Frat Pack, which included Brendan Fraser, Cole Hauser, Anthony Rapp, and Chris O'Donnell in addition to Damon and Affleck, tended to help each other out rather than run each other over in a rush to win good roles. Thus Damon did not hesitate to share the news when his agent informed him about a new movie starring Al Pacino that offered a substantial supporting role for a young actor. Everybody in the group was at about the same place professionally, and Damon knew that each of them wanted that part. He also made a point of being open about the opportunity because he believed that not only was good competition fair, but it elevated the merit of his audition should he win the role.

However, after Damon disclosed the news about the audition, his costar Chris O'Donnell was uncharacteristically disinterested. Suspicious, Damon soon found out the reason for O'Donnell's lack of enthusiasm. In a quote from Chris Nickson's *Matt Damon: An Unauthorized Biography*, Damon describes how he confronted O'Donnell about his suspicions: "I go up to Chris and say, 'Have you heard about this movie?' and he says, 'Yeah.' So I say, 'Do you have the script?' 'Yeah.' 'Can I see it?' 'No—I kinda need it.' Chris wouldn't give it to anybody." Apparently O'Donnell had heard about *Scent of a Woman* before anyone else and had kept it a secret to eliminate the competition.

O'Donnell's secrecy alienated many members of the cast and cost him several friends. Damon was among those who felt betrayed by his actions—he felt very strongly about fairness and winning a role based on his acting ability, not because there was no one else to choose from. O'Donnell had been in the movie business a little longer than the others and knew its ins and outs. He was one of the few who had a publicist to market his image to casting agents and directors. O'Donnell may not have necessarily been a better actor than the rest of the Frat Pack, but he definitely knew how to sell himself better. Although Damon and the others auditioned for the role of Charlie for *Scent of a Woman*, their performances were merely a formality. It is common practice to hold several auditions even when someone has already been chosen. Damon went ahead figuring that O'Donnell probably already had the part, and he was right. It angered him that he had not even had the chance to show his talent for such a lucrative role. From that point on, Damon considered O'Donnell a sort of professional "nemesis."

Geronimo Falls Flat

Though Damon had been so certain he was doing the right thing at the right time, the public response to *Geronimo* was disappointing. As it turned out, it was neither a commercial nor a critical success. What had happened? All the right pieces had been there—the publicity, the big names—but soon after its release the buzz just fizzled out. It was the film's stark realism and lack of emotional impact that turned audiences off and left critics shaking their heads. British magazine *Sight and Sound* had this to say in a scathing review of *Geronimo:*

> [It was] an annoying muddle . . . [that had] nothing new to say; white men speak with forked tongues and Indians are treated shamefully . . . the aim here is to simply embellish the myth. The phrase "An American Legend" in the title is a telling pointer. It allows the co-option of the real Geronimo into a patriotic scheme of things in which he represents all that is best and most endearing in the American spirit. . . . [Lieutenant Davis' story] seems shop-worn and fundamentally flawed. Davis' tedious observations diminish the Apache leader to a supporting player in his own movie. Also the fact that Davis is morally spotless—he makes a point of telling us that he didn't kill any Apaches—lets the audience off the hook.[36]

Even the best reviews called the film nothing more than a "watchable history lesson." None of the reviews had anything to say about Damon's performance as Davis, however, opting to focus on the main stars, Duvall and Hackman. The movie's acting ensemble was generally called "flat," and many audiences left theaters feeling there could have been something more to the story. In achieving its aim of telling it like it is, *Geronimo* failed to speak to its viewers' hearts.

Desperate Days

Following the dismal reception of *Geronimo* at the box office, Damon fell into a sort of depression. He was by no means debilitated by it, as he jumped at every chance to read scripts and audi-

When Damon's role as Second Lieutenant Britton Davis was soon forgotten, he questioned his decision to quit Harvard.

tion whenever his agent called. However, he was keenly aware that he had just finished a high-publicity movie with two major stars and he was no closer to success than he had been before. Damon later said of this time, "That's the frustrating thing about being an actor. It's like you're not controlling your own destiny. And I felt like I had given up college, and all these great experiences, and all my friends had graduated—I had missed out on a lot here and I was back at square one, living in L.A. It was really like a horrible feeling."[37]

For the first time, Damon did not have college to distract him from the lack of work coming his way. At least he could commiserate with roommate Ben Affleck, who had dropped out of Occidental College to act full-time as well. Besides a leading role in the comedy *Glory Daze* (1996), he was basically unemployed, too. They could barely scrape up the rent money between them sometimes, and survived on ramen noodles, Spam, and Cheerios.

One opportunity to act in a big feature did come along, however. Damon was offered a part in the Sharon Stone western *The Quick and the Dead*, but after reading the script he turned it down. Though he was not in the position to be turning down parts in high-stakes productions, Matt Damon was not about to compromise his principles for the sake of a big paycheck. He felt that the script was clichéd and the story was weak. He remembers explaining his decision to his surprised agent:

> You know what I did last night? I watched *Bullitt* [a 1968 police drama starring Steve McQueen]. Robert Duvall drives a cab in that movie, and he has, like, four lines, but he was totally believable, and he was really good, and at the end of the day he was in *Bullitt*. He's in all these great movies because he doesn't do this kind of thing [take roles in movies such as *The Quick and the Dead*].[38]

Damon wanted to act in a film that offered him the potential to really develop a character, to allow him to use his experience and skills, and to grow as an actor. Small bits that paid little also took little commitment from him, but a large part that had little potential was not worth his time. He did not want to star in another movie with big names that would easily be forgotten. Damon's instincts were right. The part went to Leonardo DiCaprio instead, and the movie ended up doing nothing for either his or Stone's careers.

Through this decision process, Damon leaned on Affleck's shoulder for support. Likewise, Affleck leaned on Damon for support too. They were united in their quest for quality scripts that offered good parts. They had not gotten into acting for the money or for public adulation. They would have been happy just to make enough to pay rent and buy food as long as they were professionally challenged and critically respected. The Hollywood glitz and glamour did not impress either one of them. The liberal values of his mother and the intellectual climate of Harvard were very much a part of what motivated Damon's principles. "Because somebody is on a television show or in a movie, does that qualify them to talk about important issues?" Damon commented. "Very few actors are moving out of their houses and getting out of their Range Rovers to pick up their fellow man."[39]

From Actor to Screenwriter

However, Damon found sticking to his principles difficult. After turning down *The Quick and the Dead*, nothing else came along. "We were frustrated," Damon later said, "because all we got to look at were the scripts everyone on the short list [the stars] passes on, then it's you and everyone else brawling for these meager table scraps."[40] The "table scraps" held few quality roles—those were difficult to come by.

Leonardo DiCaprio took the role as the kid in The Quick and the Dead *after Damon turned it down.*

After many disappointments, Damon and Affleck decided to write their own movie script.

Damon and Affleck finally concluded that if they wanted good parts they would simply have to write their own script. The script would include parts tailor-made for each of them, offering them high visibility and a chance to utilize their acting talents. They figured it would have to be an independent film, since most likely no known production company would finance a script by two unknown writers, starring two little-known actors. Damon later recalled his and Affleck's plan: "We'll raise the money on our own, and it doesn't matter if nobody sees it, 'cause when we're feeling bad, we can put this videocassette in and say, 'That's a contribution that we made to this field that we love.'"[41]

Damon and Affleck needed a story, and so they pulled out Matt's unfinished one-act play that he had written at Harvard. It was forty pages long, with well-defined characters, but the plot was not fleshed out. "We didn't touch it and one night we were just sitting there," Damon recalled. "We were kind of spitballing and then it took off."[42]

It was a learning process since neither one of them really knew how to write a screenplay. They approached the script from an actor's perspective—as scenes rather than as a whole story, with a structure from beginning to end. Damon described how they went about creating the script, usually during long drives between auditions:

> We tell each other stories while in a particular character, usually to crack each other up or to make sure that Ben doesn't fall asleep at the wheel. When we get into an improv [an unplanned act] that we both like . . . and dialogue we are relatively excited about, I will open up the glove compartment where I keep my notebook and write down a few notes that we will use later to recall the entire improvisation.[43]

They muddled through it on instinct, using each other as a sounding board for scenes that they would act out and then write down. The only problem was that the script stretched out longer and longer, with no end in sight.

On the one hand, working on the script was a blessing because it filled their empty days. Damon believes script writing was what kept him and Affleck going when they had no work. "It was like, why are we sitting here? Let's make our own movie," Damon recalled. "It beats sitting here going crazy. When you have so much energy and so much passion and no outlet for it and nobody cares, it's just the worst feeling."[44]

On the other hand, the script was growing out of control, with no real direction in the story line. The average movie script is about 120 pages; Damon and Affleck's script had grown to over a thousand pages by the end of 1993. As 1994 began, the two frustrated actor/writers began to chafe at each other. They were spending too much time together, completely focused on a piece of work that seemed to be going nowhere. Soon, however, both Damon and Affleck locked onto jobs that would get them out of each other's hair for a while. It was a break they both needed.

The Good Old Boys

It had been almost two years since he finished work on *Geronimo: An American Legend*, and Matt Damon was beginning to feel desperate again. Affleck was leaving to go back east after landing a part in Kevin Smith's production *Mallrats*, but Damon had nothing in the works yet. The only possibility was a role in a modestly budgeted production that was to be Tommy Lee Jones's directing debut. The movie, a western set in 1906 called *The Good Old Boys*, was going to be a television production, but Damon felt it was a high-quality script, and it offered him another chance to work with respected actors, including Sissy Spacek, Frances McDormand, and Sam Shepard, in addition to Jones, who would also act in the movie.

Damon's previous experience in westerns, including his ability to ride horseback, helped immensely in gaining him a role in the film. Soon Damon had left the apartment in Eagle Rock and was on his way to west Texas, where shooting for *The Good Old Boys* was to begin. He was eager to work with professionals he admired and ready to learn whatever he could from the experience. Damon was impressed with the fact that Jones was making the movie because he had a story he wanted to tell rather than because it had huge profit potential. It gave Damon confidence that art and commerce could exist together.

Damon was cast as Cotton Calloway, one of two sons of a struggling farmer who is visited by his drifting cowboy brother,

During the writing of Good Will Hunting, *Affleck worked on* Mallrats *with director Kevin Smith, left, actress Shannen Doherty, right, and actor Jason Lee, center.*

played by Jones. Cotton is a young man fascinated by machinery and the "great progress" of industry and technology. Damon's part was relatively small, but as always he dedicated himself to the role and turned out an acceptable performance.

The Good Old Boys, which aired on TNT in 1995, proved to be only a modest success, but Damon had not joined the cast with the same high expectations he had brought to *Geronimo*. He was just happy to be acting and learning from some well-respected actors. Best of all, the experience had inspired him to jump back into developing the script he and Affleck had been working on for so long.

A Script for Sale

While Affleck was still in New Jersey filming *Mallrats*, he and Damon began to fax ideas for their script back and forth. The story began to look like a thriller, as Damon described it later: "We had well over a thousand pages of these characters. We didn't know what to do with them. We had the National Security Agency taking [an] interest in [the janitor character Will's] gift [he was a genius] and wanting him for their nefarious schemes." [45] When Affleck finished work on *Mallrats*, he and Damon got a new apartment together in West Hollywood closer to the film studios. They continued to go to auditions but attacked the script with new zeal.

In October 1994 they were ready to find a producer for the film. They persuaded a friend, Chris Moore, who was working as a talent agent to read it. He loved it and immediately quit his job so that he could work full-time on raising the money to develop the script into a film he would independently produce. Still the length and structure of the script was a problem, and both Damon and Affleck knew it. They needed guidance so they gave it to Damon's agent, who showed it to the agency's literary branch.

The agency was also impressed, and to Damon and Affleck's amazement suggested they try to sell it to a studio. They had never considered that anyone would pay them for the script. Until now, making it themselves had seemed the only option. Chris Moore agreed that they should try to sell it, even though he had invested a lot of time into financing it independently.

The Real Skylar

Minnie Driver's character in *Good Will Hunting*, the medical student named Skylar, was actually based on Damon's first real girlfriend. While at Harvard he dated a girl named Skylar Satenstein, who was attending Columbia University in New York as a premed student. The two had met in New York while Damon was there auditioning. Despite the distance between them (Cambridge and New York are two hundred miles apart), they fell in love and often commuted on weekends to see each other.

However, when Damon dropped out of Harvard and moved to California, the relationship withered. The long distance made it difficult for them to visit each other, and eventually they broke it off. Skylar later graduated from medical school and went on to marry Lars Ulrich, the drummer from the rock band Metallica. Damon paid tribute to his first love by writing her character into his Academy Award–winning screenplay *Good Will Hunting*.

On November 13, 1994, the bidding for the script, which they had titled *Good Will Hunting*, began. Although they were excited at the prospect of a real Hollywood studio producing their movie, they were also concerned about retaining artistic control of the script. They had stipulated that whoever purchased it would have to agree to cast Damon and Affleck in the roles of Will Hunting and his friend Chuckie.

For four days straight, Damon and Affleck kept busy in a frenzy of meetings and phone calls, negotiating prices and contracts with various studios. Ben Affleck remembered how astounded they were by the offers: "When the phone started ringing, we were ready to take the first offer, which was $15,000." [46] To a pair of virtually unemployed actors, that amount seemed like a huge sum of money. It was, in fact, just about the same amount they had envisioned the budget for their independent production would be. But their literary agent cautioned them to be patient and hold out for more.

In the end, they accepted a bid from Castle Rock Entertainment, which had offered $600,000 for the screenplay and accepted the terms of casting Damon and Affleck in the movie. *Good Will Hunting* was actually going to be made, and the two professional partners celebrated their success. They couldn't quite believe it, as Damon later said: "We were afraid on a human level. We were talking about the difference between eating Spam every day and being able to buy a three-bedroom house with a pool table and new cars."[47] After scraping a living together for several years, they appreciated just simply being able to afford dinner out at the Sizzler. They also moved into a nicer four-bedroom house, which they rented with two other roommates.

Trouble with Castle Rock

After the sale of *Good Will Hunting*, Damon and Affleck thought it would be smooth sailing. They knew they would have to cut down the script, but they were confident of the outcome. They met with Castle Rock partner Rob Reiner and explained that they wanted the focus of the movie to be on the characters. In response, Reiner suggested they eliminate the thriller aspect and scale the story down. Affleck recalled how their vision of the story began to change:

After Castle Rock Entertainment made an offer for Good Will Hunting, *Damon and Affleck met with Rob Reiner, pictured.*

We thought we needed to insert an element that would sell the script. We were lucky enough to run into people who were smart enough to say, "You don't need that." We were reluctant at first because we thought that was what everyone was supposed to want. We figured we needed an antagonist. We didn't know that you were allowed to make a movie without a bad guy. We didn't think anyone would do that.[48]

By the end of the meeting, the script had been ripped apart and put back together again, with just sixty-three of the original pages. Damon and Affleck were put to work rewriting most of the story, this time focusing on the characters. Along the way Reiner offered suggestions, and even brought in screenwriter William Goldman for a day to give them specific guidance.

Their initial exhilaration quickly deflated as they spent their days struggling to rewrite the script. Damon had created the script in the first place so that he could act in a good role. Endless rewrites were not what he had in mind. Moreover, Castle Rock's interest in the project seemed to be fading with each submitted draft. His commitment to rewriting the script was also getting in the way of his attending auditions for other films. He did make the final cut for the part of the altar boy accused of murdering an archbishop in the film *Primal Fear* (1996), featuring Richard Gere. It was the only possible acting job he had lined up, but in the end he lost out to actor Edward Norton.

Then in the spring of 1995 Damon auditioned for a role in a high-profile movie that had already cast Meg Ryan and one of Damon's personal favorites, Denzel Washington. The movie was *Courage Under Fire*, which dealt with a story surrounding the 1991 Gulf War. Damon won a substantial supporting role, and once again he harbored hope that he would finally gain the recognition he felt he deserved for his acting.

Chapter 4

The Breakthrough

Matt Damon hoped 1995 would be the year of his breakthrough. With a supporting role in the highly publicized *Courage Under Fire*, he was certain he would be noticed by critics and the public. He wanted to prove his talent in this role, and to do that he had to put the script of *Good Will Hunting* on the back burner. When *Courage Under Fire* failed to boost his career and then Castle Rock lost interest in *Good Will Hunting*, Damon began to lose hope. But at the last minute, the script was bought by Miramax, and suddenly everything turned around for Matt Damon.

Courage Under Fire

In *Courage Under Fire*, Damon plays Ilario, a drug-addicted army medic who is haunted by his actions during the Gulf War. The plot centers around an investigation of the late Captain Karen Walden (played by Meg Ryan), who died during Operation Desert Storm after landing her helicopter to rescue a wounded U.S. chopper crew. Colonel Nat Serling (played by Denzel Washington) conducts the investigation to determine whether Walden deserves the Congressional Medal of Honor. While interviewing members of Walden's crew, Serling discovers they are hiding something. It is Ilario who finally reveals the truth of how Walden, faced with mutiny and seriously wounded, stayed behind to allow her crew to escape. Crew chief Monfriez (played by Lou Diamond Phillips), who had instigated the mutiny, feared being court-martialed and told their rescuers that Walden was dead. The crew watched as the region was napalmed, knowing Walden would die along with everything else on the ground. The burden of carrying this secret is what haunts Ilario.

Damon lost forty-one pounds for his role as drug-addicted army medic Ilario in Courage Under Fire.

During the preparation for the filming, which took place in the Texas desert near El Paso, Damon and his costars were trained by military advisers and a former medevac pilot from Desert Storm in regimentation, how to perform military duties, and daily life as a soldier. They were also trained at a firing range by the Austin, Texas SWAT team. Following the "boot camp lite," as the cast called their military training, shooting commenced for the scenes that took place during Desert Storm.

Damon was especially excited about working with Denzel Washington, whose talents he greatly respected. From the beginning of production, Washington also became one of Damon's biggest supporters. Director Ed Zwick said, "On his first day of shooting a scene with Denzel, Denzel and I looked at each other and we both knew what was registering with us—this is the real deal. There have been moments when you meet someone for the first time and their talent is immediate. When Matt walked in, it was so abundantly clear that he had the abilities."[49]

When the desert scenes were completed, Damon began preparing for the scenes in which Ilario appears after the war as a guilt-tormented junkie. Without the support of a physician, Damon went on a diet, intending to lose enough weight to look haggard. The diet resulted in his losing 41 pounds in one hundred days, and his weight plummeted to a gaunt 139 pounds. Damon later discussed the diet during an interview with Oprah Winfrey:

> I ate nothing but egg whites and chicken—and I ran 12.8 miles a day, every day—and low carbs, one baked potato to two baked potatoes a day. . . . Well, what happened at the time was I really wasn't a big enough actor for the studio to pay for a nutritionist and I didn't have the money to pay for one, so I was like, well, I'm twenty-five. I'll just do it, and so I did." [50]

Damon thought that his willingness to sacrifice his health would set him apart from other actors and make the industry take notice of his dedication to acting.

However, stripping down to less than 2 percent body fat had some effects that Damon had not bargained for. After filming his scenes as the haggard Ilario, he finally consulted a doctor, who chided Damon for his recklessness. "When the doctor . . . sat me down, he said, 'The good news is that your heart didn't shrink.' Then he ran all these tests." [51] The tests showed that Damon's adrenal gland, which controls a person's metabolism, was severely weakened. His doctor placed him on medication to ease the stress on the adrenal gland, without which he could suffer problems with weight loss, lethargy, and nausea for several years. Despite the tax to his health, Damon did not regret losing the weight, considering it just another business decision.

After the release of *Courage Under Fire*, Damon once again waited for the phone to ring. The reviews were mixed but generally good. Although Damon received some praise for his performance as Ilario, most of the attention was focused on the biggest stars, Washington and Ryan. *Variety* noted his efforts, stating, "Damon also excels as Ilario, whose upbeat spin on everything can't forever conceal the problems just beneath the surface." [52] But even this was offered as merely a sidenote to the bigger stars.

Washington did go to bat for Damon, publicly praising his acting whenever he got the chance.

However, no other film offers came, and the phone remained silent for another six months. Discouraged, Damon contemplated quitting acting for the first time. He had given his all to the part and hardly anyone had noticed. What more could he possibly do to get the recognition he felt he deserved? There was still the script of

Robert Duvall

Although Matt Damon has professed his admiration for several actors and actresses, veteran actor Robert Duvall stands out the most. Duvall is recognized for his versatility and ability to perform many roles. He is most known for his screen debut as the mysterious Boo Radley in *To Kill a Mockingbird* (1963), and for his portrayal of a ruthless television network executive in *Network* (1976). Duvall has earned several Academy Award nominations, including Best Supporting Actor for his roles in *The Godfather* (1972) and *Apocalypse Now* (1979). He won the Academy Award for Best Actor for his performance as a country music star in *Tender Mercies* (1983), which happens to be one of Damon's favorite movies.

As he was growing up, Damon watched Duvall's movies and studied the techniques he applied to the characters. He admired Duvall's willingness to choose parts based on their quality and opportunity for professional growth, a career principle that Damon later adopted.

Damon was thrilled when he had the chance to meet Duvall on the set of *Geronimo: An American Legend* in 1993. He experienced the opportunity of a lifetime: to study a master at work firsthand. Damon absorbed as much knowledge as he could. Several years later, when *Good Will Hunting* was up for a number of Academy Awards, Damon considered being nominated for Best Actor alongside Duvall a greater honor than the nomination itself.

Damon studied Duvall's movies to learn acting techniques.

Costars Michael Moriarty and Denzel Washington, at right. Washington recognized Damon's talent on the set of Courage Under Fire.

Good Will Hunting, but he was beginning to wonder if that dream, too, was floundering.

Castle Rock Bows Out

Damon and Affleck had suspected for some time that Castle Rock was losing interest in their script. (They had submitted draft after draft but received little or no comments.) Before Damon had left for Texas to film *Courage Under Fire*, he and Affleck had continued faxing ideas for the script back and forth. In an attempt to get Castle Rock's attention, they began writing absurd scenes into the script, such as making Will's psychiatrist into a construction foreman instead. When this received no response, they decided to insert a lewd one-liner in the dialogue between two of the characters, certain that if anyone at Castle Rock was reading the script, the line would be censored. When this draft too came back with no comments, they increased the section. "The sequence had grown from one line to, like, three lines," Damon later said, "and by the end it's almost a paragraph, and they never said anything about it. We thought it would be a little inside joke. And when they didn't notice, it was just sad."[53]

After Damon finished *Courage Under Fire*, it became clear that he and Affeck were going to have to fight Castle Rock for more than just revisions of the script of *Good Will Hunting*. When Castle Rock informed them that the movie was to be filmed in Toronto, they protested. They were adamant that it needed to be done in Boston, where the story takes place, in order to retain its flavor and realism. To Damon and Affleck, Boston was another character in the story. To eliminate it would have stripped the movie of its authenticity. Toronto was less expensive, Castle Rock explained. Damon and Affleck adamantly refused to agree to this proposal. In addition, they were not happy with Castle Rock's choice of director, Andrew Scheinman. Scheinman had directed the comedy *Little Big League* (1994), but Damon and Affleck felt that these credentials did not qualify him for directing the film that they had poured their souls into. Soon, meetings with Castle Rock disintegrated into arguments over their differences.

The problems between Damon and Affleck and Castle Rock led the production company to finally put *Good Will Hunting* in "turnaround," which meant that Damon and Affleck had the opportunity to sell their script to another company within thirty days. If they could not sell it in thirty days, Castle Rock would retain the script and could use it however it wished. To complicate the process, the script was now worth $1 million because of the development costs the production company had already invested in the work. This price scared off many potential buyers, and rumors circulated within the industry that Damon and Affleck were "difficult" to work with. All through November 1995 they waited anxiously for someone to snatch up *Good Will Hunting*, knowing that if it failed to sell, their dreams and hard work would amount to nothing. Castle Rock told them that if they could not sell the script, neither of them would be cast in the film, and they would be lucky if they received tickets to the premiere.

Miramax Saves the Day

On the twenty-seventh day of turnaround, Affleck decided to show the script to Kevin Smith, the director of the film he was working on, *Chasing Amy* (1997). Smith took it home and read it that night. He was so moved by the story that the next morning he went straight to the cochairman of Miramax Pictures, Harvey Weinstein. Damon later described how Smith "saved" the script:

> Miramax originally passed on the script [when they first sold it] because Harvey Weinstein never read it. And Ben was doing *Chasing Amy* with Kevin . . . and Kevin read the script because Ben was . . . living on his couch. It was Kevin who had a deal at Miramax and called Harvey, and said, "You have to read this script." Harvey read it, and two days later we were at Miramax. If not for Kevin Smith, the movie would have gone to Castle Rock, and we would have been cut out of it. That title [coexecutive producer of *Good Will Hunting*] doesn't say what Kevin did—which was save our butts.[54]

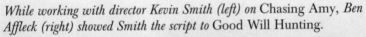

While working with director Kevin Smith (left) on Chasing Amy, *Ben Affleck (right) showed Smith the script to* Good Will Hunting.

Weinstein's offer was for just under $1 million. The following month Damon and Affleck received another big surprise. En route to Boston, they received a call from Weinstein informing them that actor and director Mel Gibson was interested in directing *Good Will Hunting*. They had to be in New York to meet with him in just two days. Although the meeting went very well, Gibson confessed that he would not be able to begin production for another year because of his commitment to act in *Ransom* (1996). Damon and Affleck did not want to wait another year to do their film, which was already years in the making. As much as they admired and respected Gibson, they were adamant about the time issue. As a result, Gibson was forced to decline the opportunity to direct *Good Will Hunting*.

It was not long before Damon wondered whether they should have waited for Gibson. Without a big-name director or cast member, the film continued to sit on the back burner. To make things worse, Damon had no other work as 1996 dawned. Even Affleck found work in Marc Pellington's *Going All the Way* (1997), leaving Damon to sit around alone and depressed in their cheap New York apartment, where they had moved to be closer to Boston for the future production of *Good Will Hunting*. He wondered again whether he should quit acting for a while and finish up his Harvard education.

Soon after, however, Damon's agent called with the news that he needed to be on the next available flight to Memphis, Tennessee, for an audition the following day for the lead role in *John Grisham's The Rainmaker*. It should have been a dream come true for Damon, who had always wanted the chance to work with the film's director, Francis Ford Coppola. However, Damon knew that the fact he was being called in at the last minute was merely to make the audition look bigger than it was. In fact, he had heard that fellow actor Edward Norton had already filled the lead role.

A Breakthrough

Nevertheless, Damon went to Memphis. Since he didn't have a script to review for the audition, Damon took a copy of the novel *The Rainmaker* along for the plane trip, reading it to soak up the nuances of the lead character, young lawyer Rudy Baylor. The next morning he was finally handed a script, which he studied furiously. The part he was auditioning for called for a Southern accent, which Damon, being a Boston boy, did not have. He could, however, imitate one, as he later explained: "Luckily, my girlfriend at the time [model Kara Sands] was from Texas. I could do *her* accent, so I basically imitated her. It's different from a Knox County [Tennessee] accent but, still, it was close. So I threw together this kind of haphazard performance." [55] Damon's audition opposite Claire Danes, who had already been cast in the film, went well, but he remained skeptical about the outcome.

Nearly two weeks after the audition, Damon was offered the part. (He did not discover until later that Edward Norton *had* originally been cast as Rudy Baylor, but he had bowed out of the project after falling ill.) It was finally happening: a lead role in a highly publicized feature, with a big name director. The industry could no longer ignore Matt Damon on the screen.

Good Will Hunting Takes Off

Damon's high-profile role in *The Rainmaker* was also indirectly responsible for the film industry's renewed interest in *Good Will Hunting*. Damon realized right away that this was the push that might get big names interested in *Good Will Hunting*. "The day after I got *The Rainmaker*, I sent Harvey Weinstein a fax," recalled Damon. "We'd been trying to get *Good Will* done for a year, and I said, 'Dear Harvey, I *am* the Rainmaker, I'm that guy.' He called back and said, 'All right, I'll call you.'" [56]

Shortly thereafter, Weinstein did call, with the news that Gus Van Sant was interested in directing *Good Will Hunting*. Van Sant was known for making critically acclaimed independent films outside the Hollywood mainstream, including *Drugstore Cowboy* (1989) and the 1995 hit *To Die For*. Miramax believed that Van Sant was a perfect choice to direct *Good Will Hunting*. He could make a sentimental story with a dark edge without veering too much in either direction. Both Damon and Affleck were impressed by Van Sant's enthusiasm for the film, and they felt at ease handing him the reins, as Damon later explained: "The most important step was giving up the script and handing it to Gus and saying, 'This is your movie

Matt Damon's Leading Ladies

Although Matt Damon has been romantically linked with several actresses, including Claire Danes (on the set of *The Rainmaker*), perhaps
his most well known romance was with his *Good Will Hunting* costar
Minnie Driver. The chemistry between them was obvious from the moment Driver auditioned for the part of Skylar. Damon admitted in Chris
Nickson's book *Matt Damon: An Unauthorized Biography* that part of
Driver's allure was the awe her talent inspired in him: "Min is just an ex-
traordinary actress—she's like the best actress I know. [She says] everything from 'Let's do this' to 'Let's try this scene here'—the rehearsal
process was amazing to watch her work."

They continued to see each other throughout the summer of 1997 when
Damon was in England filming *Saving Private Ryan* and Driver was nearby
working on her new film *The Governess* (1998). In England they had appeared to be a tight-knit couple, and for some time after Damon returned
to the United States they continued to be an item in the public eye.

However, behind the scenes, Damon had begun to date actress Winona
Ryder. His breakup with Driver did not become public knowledge until
he announced it during an interview on *Oprah*. On the air Damon admitted, "Well, I'm single. I was with Minnie for a while, but we're not
romantically involved anymore. We're just really good friends. . . . We
care about each other a lot. We just decided it wasn't meant to be."
Many people assumed Damon had dumped Driver right there on *Oprah*,
despite his insistence that the breakup was mutual. He later regretted
the announcement.

Since the public uproar ignited
by his statements about his
breakup with Driver, keeping
his relationships private has
become a matter of principle
for Damon. Bob Strauss, a film
writer for the *L.A. Daily News*,
quoted Damon, who said, "I
still talk, obviously, about my
personal life with the people
who I'm close with and I trust.
It was a quick change; I realized, once that happened a
couple of years ago, how not to
go about it."

*At one time, Damon was
romantically involved with actress
Winona Ryder.*

When Gus Van Sant, pictured here, signed on to direct Good Will Hunting, *Damon and Affleck developed confidence in the production of the film.*

now.' We had to have a director who was going to heighten it and make it better, otherwise the film would have been a total failure for us." [57]

The choice of Van Sant as director was not the only big name to catapult the film into action. Soon after Van Sant signed on, veteran actor Robin Williams expressed his interest in playing the part of Sean McGuire, the psychologist who ultimately helps Will Hunting. Williams had loved the script and wanted the opportunity to work with Van Sant. Williams explained why he was so impressed with the script:

> This script wasn't a diamond in the rough—it was a diamond in the setting. It was already there. The dialogue worked. Coming from how young Matt and Ben are, it's amazing the depth of experience they've been able to capture. The stuff they talk about, normally you'd think you would have to go through a lot more to be able to talk about it that personally. [58]

Having Robin Williams sign as a member of the cast was the final push that Miramax needed. With a popular and critically acclaimed star like Williams participating, the film was almost guaranteed to be made.

Despite all the action buzzing around *Good Will Hunting*, somehow Damon managed to break himself away to concentrate on making *The Rainmaker* during the fall and early winter of 1996.

John Grisham's The Rainmaker

In his typical fashion, Damon prepared to *become* Rudy Baylor. Since the character of Rudy is from Knoxville, he moved to Knoxville, Tennessee, and got a job as a bartender during the summer of 1996. He made friends who introduced him to the daily activities of the average Knoxville resident, including going to pubs, jazz clubs, and the local high school football games. He also picked up the accents and social subtleties of the region. In particular, he found the behavior of the traditional Southern gentleman easy to pick up thanks to his mother. She had brought Damon up to respect women, and he knew how to charm using eye contact and smiles. He also spent time in Memphis because Rudy attends law school in Memphis. Damon even paid attention to minute details such as the differences between the Memphis and Knoxville accents. "Knoxville's a lot twangier; Memphis is a lot more subtle, more like how John Grisham talks. So I wanted him to be kind of losing that Knoxville accent."[59] It is this eye to detail that allows Damon to create the authenticity of his characters. Although most viewers probably did not notice outright, Damon used the accent differences to add dimension to Rudy's character in particular scenes. For example, in emotional scenes, he would revert to the Knoxville accent of Rudy's upbringing, but in other instances he implied Rudy's growing sense of confidence by using the Memphis accent.

Once filming began on the set of *The Rainmaker*, Damon felt he was prepared to flesh out the character of Rudy on the screen. He was, however, acutely aware that this production was not like any other he had ever been part of. Although he had been in a couple of highly publicized features that had allowed him to work with some big name stars, for the first time he found his own name listed above theirs in the credits. Instead of inflating his ego, this fueled his desire to turn out the best performance of his career. He was doing what he loved to do with colleagues who he admired and his goal was simply to do his part to make the film a success.

Although Coppola initially intimidated him, Damon soon learned that the director's intention was to guide him, and all the actors, into turning out their best performances. Damon described Coppola as "constantly trying [to keep the actors] on their toes. His theory is that in life, you don't know what's going to happen next, so why in a movie should you know you're going to say this, walk there, hit that mark? It should be more spontaneous and unplanned."[60] Coppola encouraged improvisation and sometimes surprised the cast by playing practical jokes on the set. This approach kept the dialogue fresh and the actors on their toes.

Damon also had the opportunity to learn from his well-seasoned costars on and off the set. These colleagues included Danny DeVito, Jon Voight, Mickey Rourke, Virginia Madsen, and Danny Glover. One costar he especially admired was Teresa Wright, the

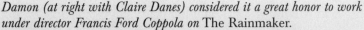

Damon (at right with Claire Danes) considered it a great honor to work under director Francis Ford Coppola on The Rainmaker.

During the filming of The Rainmaker, *Damon was honored to work with Academy Award–winning actress Teresa Wright.*

1942 Academy Award–winning actress for *Mrs. Miniver*. Wright, who played Miss Birdie in *The Rainmaker*, had achieved the kind of career Damon wanted—the respected actor whose work spanned more than fifty years and who was still remembered for her artistic excellence. That was the legacy that Matt Damon wanted to leave behind.

Damon's role in *The Rainmaker* gave him much more screen-time than he had had in previous roles. In the movie, Rudy Baylor has just graduated from law school and has no job and no place to live. A shady lawyer takes him under his wing and assigns him to work with Deck Schifflet (played by DeVito), who teaches Rudy the essentials of ambulance chasing (soliciting work from people who have suffered injuries, accidents, or conflicts with health insurance companies). Among Rudy's first clients are the Blacks, whose son is dying of leukemia. The Blacks are suing their insurance company for refusing to pay for their son's treatments. Damon's character also becomes involved with Kelly Riker (played by Claire Danes), a victim of domestic abuse who eventually kills her husband in self-defense. In the end Rudy proves in the courtroom that the insurance company has defrauded its clients, and the Blacks are awarded substantial damages. In a twist, however, they later learn that the company has declared bankruptcy and the Blacks will probably never see their money. Disillusioned, Rudy quits the law and leaves town with Kelly, uncertain of his future.

After the filming of *The Rainmaker* was finished, Damon went back to Boston to begin production of *Good Will Hunting*. He had appreciated the opportunity to work with Coppola and was grateful for the publicity his role in *The Rainmaker* had brought him, but his heart was in Boston, where his longtime dream was about to become a reality.

Chapter 5

The Making of a Star

MATT DAMON HAD high hopes for the success of both *Good Will Hunting* and *The Rainmaker*. He was finally going to have the chance to show the film industry and moviegoers the kind of acting he was capable of. Most of all he hoped people would enjoy *Good Will Hunting* and that he would receive the critical recognition that would get directors fighting to cast him. Little did he know just how far *The Rainmaker* and *Good Will Hunting* would catapult his career.

The Making of *Good Will Hunting*

The first order of business was casting the rest of the film's roles, with two substantial supporting roles still to be decided. In New York, auditions were held for the part of Skylar, Will's medical student love interest. The first actress to audition with Damon was Minnie Driver, who had turned out an excellent performance in *Circle of Friends* (1996). The chemistry between her and Damon during the audition was so electrifying that the director and producers were moved to tears. There was no question that Minnie Driver *was* Skylar. The other role was for Gerald Lambeau, the professor who mentored Will Hunting, which eventually went to a rising Swedish actor, Stellan Skarsgård.

Although Damon and Affleck were involved with the initial preparation and casting, it was not until the first day of shooting that they were hit with the realization that their movie was finally being made. Since Robin Williams was the biggest star and he had a very tight schedule, the film's shooting revolved around him. The first scene involved Williams, Damon, and Affleck. "By the time they said 'action' tears were running down my face," Damon

Ben Affleck: Matt Damon's Alter Ego

Most people know that Ben Affleck is Matt Damon's best friend and the cowriter of their Oscar-winning screenplay *Good Will Hunting*. Affleck has been Damon's main support and creative partner ever since the two were Little League players growing up in Cambridge, Massachusetts. It is virtually impossible to tell Damon's story without telling Affleck's too.

Affleck was born in Berkeley, California, but his parents moved to Cambridge when he was still a toddler. Ever since he landed his first acting job, as a regular on the PBS series *The Voyage of the Mimi*, at the age of eight, Affleck has always worked as an actor.

After high school, small parts in television and film paid the rent, even when Damon went long stretches with no work at all. Affleck earned roles in the television miniseries *Hands of a Stranger* and Danielle Steele's *Daddy* before he and Damon were cast in *School Ties*.

His first major film appearance was as a high school bully in *Dazed and Confused* in 1993. Since his career took off with *Good Will Hunting*, Affleck has concentrated primarily on independent films and action movies. He appeared in *Armageddon* with Bruce Willis in 1998 and the independent film *200 Cigarettes*. In *Boiler Room* he played a shady Long Island stockbroker caught up in capitalistic greed.

Most recently, Affleck has starred in several mainstream films. He costarred with Sandra Bullock in the romantic comedy *Forces of Nature* and appeared with Charlize Theron and Gary Sinise in the action flick *Reindeer Games*. He has also teamed up twice with his on-again, off-again girlfriend, actress Gwyneth Paltrow, in the Oscar-winning romantic comedy *Shakespeare in Love* in 1998 and *Bounce*, which was released in theaters in November 2000.

Long before the success of Good Will Hunting, *Affleck and Damon were each other's support and inspiration.*

remembered. "I looked over at Ben, and he was the same way. Then right after the scene, Robin came over and put his hands on our heads and said, 'It's not a fluke; you guys really did it.'"[61]

The filming of *Good Will Hunting* went very smoothly. In fact the only real conflicts happened off the set and were between Van Sant and producer Lawrence Bender, who argued over creative differences. However, even this issue worked itself out, and on the set everyone worked comfortably together. Williams brought his insatiable humor to the set, putting everyone at ease and creating a jovial atmosphere. He was known for teasing Damon and Affleck, joking about their youth by asking for their identification, and sometimes screaming, "It's Matt, it's Ben. He's so hot. Oh!!"[62] For their part, Damon and Affleck enjoyed showing Williams around Boston, including the working-class neighborhoods of South Boston where the story takes place.

Filling out the experience was the presence of family and friends on and off the set. Both Casey Affleck, Ben's brother, and Cole

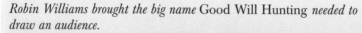

Robin Williams brought the big name Good Will Hunting *needed to draw an audience.*

Damon and Affleck invited former costars Cole Hauser, left, and Casey Affleck, second to left, to play their friends in Good Will Hunting.

Hauser, a friend and former *School Ties* costar, had supporting roles in the movie, making every day on the set like a family reunion. There is even one scene in the movie where Damon and Affleck's parents and their former high school teacher Larry Aaronson act as extras in the background. Once the Boston scenes were complete, filming moved to Toronto, where the indoor scenes would be shot.

While shooting the film, both Damon and Affleck encountered an unexpected hurdle. They both occasionally lost sense of the impact of the dialogue—a dialogue they had written and acted out themselves numerous times. Damon had worked with it for so many years and was so familiar with it that it was almost jaded in his perspective. "We'd say, 'Remember, it used to be funny, dude. It was funny once!' You gotta take that risk."[63] He struggled to regain his focus and with great concentration brought sincerity and emotion to his lines.

All too soon, the seven weeks of filming *Good Will Hunting* were over. After Van Sant went to California to edit the movie, both Damon and Affleck felt the sadness that comes with the end of a good book. Damon described his feelings: "I realize I'm not going to get up and go to work with Gus and Robin and Ben and Minnie. There's a little sadness there. But at the same time, it feels good to have [*Good Will Hunting*] done. I don't think I could ever tire of talking about it." [64]

The Hollywood Buzz

Although Damon was sorry to see the production of *Good Will Hunting* end, he and Affleck eagerly anticipated the film's release. Both *John Grisham's The Rainmaker* and *Good Will Hunting* were scheduled to premiere within weeks of each other, and the fact that Damon was starring in both caught the media's eye. Moreover, starring in two high-profile films allowed Damon to have a publicist to market his talent in magazines, newspapers, and on daytime talk shows. The more the public found out about Damon, the more they wanted to know. Newspapers and magazines were suddenly vying for the attention of both Damon and Affleck. The fact that childhood friends had written a script together and managed to get it directed by a respected veteran like Van Sant sounded like a story for a movie in itself. Damon found himself soaring from obscurity to almost star status in a matter of days. Magazines such as *Vanity Fair, US,* and *Interview* invited Damon to be their cover stories, and he shared the cover of *Premiere* with Affleck. Even before *Good Will Hunting* was released, the public was seeing his face on the covers of magazines all over the nation. It was just the sort of publicity he—and *Good Will Hunting*—needed. Moviegoers developed a curiosity about Damon, which would eventually translate into commercial revenue. Suddenly Damon was getting everything he had ever wanted—attention and respect for his acting— but it nearly overwhelmed him. Damon explained his fears in an interview before the release of *Good Will Hunting:*

> It's like I'm living someone else's life. I don't have an apartment; my stuff is in a warehouse in New Jersey. I'm making three movies in a row for all this money. . . . I'm not complaining, you know. But I mean, why is it all happening to me? And if people are expecting this much, will they be mad if I let them down? I don't want to be a flash in the pan. I don't want to lose it all. [65]

Damon knew all too well how the rising star today could end up tomorrow's forgotten has-been. He embraced the publicity but re-

Damon received great reviews for his role as attorney Rudy Baylor in John Grisham's The Rainmaker.

mained skeptical. Damon would not rest easy until the reviews for *The Rainmaker*, and especially *Good Will Hunting*, were out.

The Premieres

The Rainmaker premiered in mid-November 1997 amid much fanfare. Commercially the film was a big hit, since many people were eager to see another book by the popular lawyer-turned-novelist John Grisham come to life on the big screen. Although some critics dismissed *The Rainmaker* as just another story about how the little guy gets the big bad corporation in the end, both Coppola's directing and Damon's acting were singled out for praise. In the *New York Times*, critic Janet Maslin wrote,

> The filmmaker and the cast apparently put a great deal of effort into developing individual performances, and the result is a rich, lifelike texture for the whole film. Mr. Damon provides much of this, giving Rudy a quiet authority and courtliness. . . . Though the prototypical Grisham nice young man is by now a cliché, Mr. Damon is fresh and pensive here in ways that reinvent the character.[66]

Critics praised Damon for his ability to show how his character evolved from an uncertain kid to a strong-principled professional.

Damon demonstrated Rudy's emotional development from beginning to end using nuances such as eye contact, body posture, and even clothing.

The success of *The Rainmaker* fueled Damon's hopes for *Good Will Hunting*, which premiered in December 1997. Much to Damon's delight, it grossed $10.3 million its first weekend, more than any other movie playing at the time except the monumental *Titanic*. It continued its trend of commercial success, but the greatest satisfaction for Damon was the largely favorable critical reviews. Janet Maslin of the *New York Times* praised the script:

> Two young actors with soaring reputations have written themselves a smart and touching screenplay, then seen it directed with style, shrewdness, and clarity by Gus Van Sant. There couldn't be a better choice than the unsentimental Van Sant for material like this. . . . The script's bare bones are familiar, yet the film also has fine acting, steady momentum, a sharp eye and a very warm heart. . . . Damon, very much the supernova, is mercurial [unpredictably changeable] in ways that keep his character steadily surprising.[67]

The *Hollywood Reporter* noted the film's subtleties, including the "varied, wisely textured subplots. . . . The best thing about *Good Will Hunting* is not in its well-crafted, psychological symmetries but in the just-plain messiness of its humanity. It's rowdy, it's funny, it's heartbreaking—it rings of life."[68]

In addition to the positive reviews for the film, Damon's acting was singled out. A review in *Daily Variety* reported that "Damon gives a charismatic performance in a demanding role that's bound to catapult him to stardom. Perfectly cast, he makes the aching, step-by-step transformation of Will realistic and credible."[69]

Before long, rumors about Academy Award nominations began to surface regarding Damon's performance, the screenplay, and the film as best picture. Damon protested when asked about the rumors, unconvinced that a newcomer like him might gain such a measure of success. Being nominated for an Academy Award, the most prestigious honor in the film industry, would mean the validation of his acting abilities among his most respected colleagues. The possibility of achieving this level of respect, however, was almost too much for Damon to believe. He remained skeptical of his success. "It's totally overwhelming," Damon said. "It's a little nerve-racking, because I think the next few months are going to play a big part in what happens in my life and what course my life takes. The buzz is great. What does that mean? It could all go away, so I'm trying to keep a level head about it."[70] Damon soon found reason to throw the skepticism away.

The Golden Globe Awards

Each year in the month of January, the Golden Globe Awards are held. Long considered an accurate precursor to the Academy Awards, the Golden Globes are highly respected in their own right. In early January 1998, Damon learned that the Golden Globes had nominated him for Best Actor, Affleck for Best Supporting Actor, and both for Best Original Screenplay. This was an unexpected bonus to Damon, coming on the heels of winning the Special Award in Filmmaking from the National Board of Review in New York City, a highly respected film board consisting of critics, educators, and writers.

Damon and Affleck were ecstatic to win Best Original Screenplay for Good Will Hunting *at the 1998 Golden Globe Awards.*

The 1998 Golden Globes were held on January 18. With competition from such respected veterans as Peter Fonda and Jack Nicholson, Damon held little illusion that he might win Best Actor. Affleck likewise was doubtful of winning; he was up against Burt Reynolds, who had turned out an excellent performance in *Boogie Nights*. They were right in their assessments of their individually nominated categories. However, they felt they stood a good chance of winning for Best Original Screenplay. Sure enough, when the winners were announced, Matt Damon and Ben Affleck were named to go onstage. Winning was beyond their wildest dreams, yet here they were sharing awards with some of the actors they had looked up to and respected for years. Just a few weeks later, however, even this honor would be topped.

The Academy Awards

On February 10, 1998, the Academy Award nominations were announced. To Damon's amazement, *Good Will Hunting* reeled in a total of nine nominations, including Best Picture, Gus Van Sant for Best Director, Robin Williams for Best Supporting Actor, Minnie

At the Academy Awards, Good Will Hunting *was nominated for nine Oscars. Damon was nominated for Best Actor, Minnie Driver for Best Supporting Actress, and Gus Van Sant for Best Director.*

Driver for Best Supporting Actress, and the categories of editing, song, and original dramatic score. In addition, Damon was nominated for Best Actor, and he and Affleck once again shared the nomination for Best Original Screenplay. When he heard of the nominations, Damon admitted, "I am staggered just to have two nominations, one with my best friend and another in the company that I am in [fellow nominees Jack Nicholson, Peter Fonda, Dustin Hoffman, and Robert Duvall]. I can't even comprehend this. I already win, just being nominated."[71] Damon's joy was dampened, however, when ugly rumors began to surface just prior to the event.

In early March, Damon learned that someone had begun circulating stories regarding the origin of the script for *Good Will Hunting*. There were actually three different rumors, only one of which seemed even a little credible. One story claimed that Damon and Affleck had purchased the script from someone else, and another alleged that William Goldman, a veteran screenwriter, had been the real creator of the script. The third and most damaging story was that the script, which Damon had originally written as a one-act play, had been previously performed. The allegation was serious enough to warrant an investigation, because if the script had been performed or otherwise published prior to making the movie, it would be ineligible for the Best Original Screenplay category.

Damon and Affleck easily discredited the first two rumors. In fact, since the film's premiere in December, Damon had been forthcoming about the fact that he had purchased only the title to the script, which he had obtained from a friend who had written an unpublished novel of the same name. William Goldman had given the pair nothing more than advice during a day they spent together consulting with him on the development of the script. As for the third story, Damon insisted that his original one-act play had been acted out in class at Harvard, but it had never been performed as a theater production. In addition, there was no evidence that it had ever been previously performed or published before Castle Rock bought the script. Ben Affleck issued a statement on the World Wide Web discrediting the allegations:

> Matt and I wrote the script from beginning to end. We sat down with William Goldman for an afternoon and chatted.

. . . Here is the simple fact: People are fighting like mad over credit for various screenplays [so] why wouldn't they come forward. . . ? I have the handwritten various drafts from beginning to end at home. We wrote it. That's all. But I take it as a backhanded compliment that people are so incredulous.[72]

The writers' branch executive committee of the Academy of Motion Picture Arts and Sciences investigated the stories and found no evidence to support them. Although the rumors were put to rest before the Academy Awards ceremony took place, Damon worried about the influence the false implications might have on *Good Will Hunting*'s chances of winning.

The 70th Annual Academy Awards were held at the Dorothy Chandler Pavilion in Los Angeles on March 23, 1998. Damon and Affleck both chose to escort their mothers rather than their girlfriends (Winona Ryder and Gwyneth Paltrow, respectively) as a show of respect for the women who they felt were most responsible for helping them achieve their dreams. Although she detested the Hollywood glamour and warned Damon that she probably would dislike the experience, Nancy Carlsson-Paige wanted to support her son's endeavors. She would find much to be proud of in her son that night.

Damon knew that it would be difficult for *Good Will Hunting* to defeat the formidable *Titanic.* Just when everyone thought *Titanic* would sweep the Oscars, Robin Williams won the award for Best Supporting Actor. Damon did not expect to win Best Actor, up against notables like Jack Nicholson, Peter Fonda, Dustin Hoffman, and Robert Duvall, one of his idols. He was on top of the world just being in their company. Ultimately, he was not disappointed when Nicholson was named as the winner for his performance in *As Good As It Gets.*

After receiving the Golden Globe for their script, however, Damon would have been disappointed about leaving the Academy Awards empty-handed. The screenplay of *Good Will Hunting* was competing with those from *As Good As It Gets, Boogie Nights, Deconstructing Harry,* and *The Full Monty.* Then the unthinkable happened. Matt Damon and Ben Affleck were announced as

At the Academy Awards, Damon and Affleck won an Oscar for Best Original Screenplay.

the winners for Best Original Screenplay. In shock they hugged family and cast members and ran up onstage to give their thirty-second speeches. After breathlessly trying to name everyone they wanted to thank (including the city of Boston), they were whisked away backstage and greeted by a horde of reporters. Affleck did most of the talking because Damon was still in such a state of shock he could barely speak. Affleck summed up the experience for both of them, saying, "Matt and I thought we could raise a little money and make the movie. [But] we never thought it could go through the regular Hollywood channels."[73]

Other Awards

The Academy and Golden Globe Awards were not the only honors Damon received in 1998. In February he was named the ShoWest male winner of the Future Faces, a competition that selects a male and female "star of tomorrow." He also won a Special Achievement Award in writing and acting from the Berlin Film Festival. This honor held special meaning to Damon because it meant respect from Europe, the home of cinema. Finally, Damon was nominated for Actor in a Leading Role for the Screen Actors Guild Awards, but he did not win.

Damon was happy that his colleagues respected his work enough to honor him with awards, but the real prize for him was the power his newfound success gave him. Suddenly he was being handed scripts to read and could afford to pick and choose until he found something he liked. Moreover, he could be picky about his roles now that the directors were coming to him with offers, instead of him having to audition for lead roles. "The funny thing is," Damon said in 1997, "that as soon as you get big, the studios send you these scripts that they've been trying to get made for 20 years, that were originally written for Dustin Hoffman. They've been sitting on the shelf. You get their old standbys."[74] Matt Damon had become one of the busiest actors in Hollywood almost overnight.

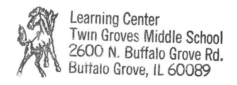

Chapter 6

Hollywood Golden Boy

MATT DAMON HAS continued to choose roles based on their quality and opportunity for professional growth rather than their potential for commercial success. In the years following his success with *Good Will Hunting* he has sometimes been criticized for taking too high a risk, gambling his career with roles that are not always "likable" or politically correct. Since 1998 Damon has taken on six major roles, some of which won public acclaim and some of which did not, but all offered him a personal and professional challenge.

Saving Private Ryan

One of the ways in which Damon fulfills his desire for a professional challenge is to secure roles in films being made by directors he greatly admires. He believes that a good director can do more than help actors bring out the best in their abilities; they can also challenge actors to stretch these abilities. That's why Damon wanted to be a part of director Steven Spielberg's World War II project *Saving Private Ryan*.

Damon had heard about *Saving Private Ryan* while working on *The Rainmaker*. Since he could not break away from *The Rainmaker* to audition for Spielberg, Damon sent him a compilation of his filmwork on tape. The audition tape included mostly his work in *Courage Under Fire*, which Damon hoped would impress Spielberg. With his leading roles in two high-profile movies, he felt somewhat confident of his chance to obtain a role in *Saving Private Ryan*. He was dumbfounded when he learned he had been rejected. After all his hard work and recent success, Damon was at a loss as to what could have gone wrong.

Damon secured his role as Private Ryan in the film Saving Private Ryan *after meeting with Steven Spielberg and Robin Williams for lunch.*

A few months later, Damon found out why he had not been chosen for a part in *Saving Private Ryan.* While he was busy shooting *Good Will Hunting* in Boston, costar Robin Williams decided to have lunch with Steven Spielberg, who happened to be in Boston at the same time filming the drama *Amistad* (1997). Spielberg and Williams were old friends, and Williams invited Damon to come along and introduce himself to the legendary director. Damon was still reeling from the disappointment of the rejection, but his admiration for Spielberg outweighed his doubts and he went along excited to meet yet another of his director idols.

During the lunch, Williams praised Damon's acting abilities, and Spielberg suddenly remembered his face from the audition tape he had sent a few months earlier. "He said, 'Do I know you?'" Damon explained. "'Are you the guy from [*Courage Under Fire*]?' And I said, yeah. He said, 'Did you gain some weight?'"[75]

It turned out that Spielberg had rejected Damon only because he wanted someone more muscular than he had appeared in the audition tape. Damon explained to Spielberg that he had lost forty pounds for his role as Ilario. "Steven thought that I still looked like I did in *Courage Under Fire.* When he actually saw me, he saw that I didn't look that way anymore, and that's what made the difference." [76] To his delight, a few days after the lunch, Damon learned that Spielberg wanted him for the title role in *Saving Private Ryan.*

During the summer of 1997, Damon joined the cast of *Saving Private Ryan* in England. Because he had been finishing *Good Will Hunting,* he had missed the "boot camp" training Spielberg had made everyone else undergo. By the time Damon arrived, the cast, which had suffered several sleepless nights in wet, cold uniforms and spent their rainy days walking six miles, was in a foul mood. "They'd been wading through mud puddles and sleeping face-down in water, and here I show up all prim and proper and ready to go. They were like, 'Why . . . did this kid not have to come to boot camp?'" [77] Ironically, the initial conflict between Damon and the cast paralleled the antagonism felt between Private Ryan and the soldiers who had to save him in the film.

Director Steven Spielberg (center) with the cast of Saving Private Ryan.

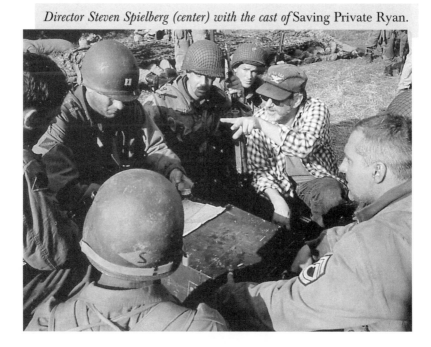

As always, Damon approached his work with *Saving Private Ryan* as an educational opportunity. He studied Spielberg's techniques, hoping to learn more about the art of filmmaking. Damon even tagged along behind him on the set one day and was amazed to see the vast amount of work that went into directing, including script changes, decisions about the lighting and angles to use during a scene shoot, editing and changing scenes, and guiding the actors through the shoots. He could barely keep up with Spielberg as he rushed from one area of the set to another.

Saving Private Ryan stars Tom Hanks, but Damon plays the title role, that of Private Ryan, the last surviving son of a family

Fighting for Janitors

Matt Damon and Ben Affleck returned to their hometown of Cambridge, Massachusetts, in May 2000 to support a Harvard rally organized to promote a pay raise for the Ivy League university's janitors. When Cambridge city councilwoman and childhood classmate Marjorie Decker asked the two actors to participate in the rally, neither hesitated. Damon, who had portrayed a janitor at MIT in *Good Will Hunting*, welcomed the opportunity to make a positive change at his former college. Affleck had personal reasons for supporting the pay raise, since both his father and stepmother had worked as janitors.

The duo's appearance at the rally attracted a huge crowd, who listened intently to the messages that Damon and Affleck expressed. In an article in *Nation* called "Unfair Harvard," Damon was quoted as saying, "This is the richest university in the world, and the fact that the people who keep the machine running—who feed the students, look out for their safety and clean their bathrooms and hallways—are not given a living wage is demeaning to us all."

Despite his comfortable upbringing, Damon's mother instilled a deep sense of fairness and equality in her son. An awareness of the informal class divisions that haunted the Boston area allowed him to recognize the Harvard pay raise conflict as symptomatic of this division.

The Harvard students' Living Wage Campaign argued that paying janitors $6.50 per hour during a booming economy was unfair. They wanted the minimum wage raised to $10.25 per hour. Harvard officials, however, defended the salary structure. Although the rally failed to convince school officials, they were very impressed with the turnout to the rally, admitting it was the largest one ever held thanks to Damon and Affleck's presence.

whose other three sons had already died in World War II. Although he appears only in the last hour of the movie, his is a highly visible role.

Released in the summer of 1998, *Saving Private Ryan* earned excellent reviews, and Damon was praised as a member of the supporting cast. Although Hanks, as the primary star, garnered most of the attention, Damon was grateful just to be a part of a successful Spielberg movie.

Rounders

Before *Saving Private Ryan* premiered, however, Damon was at work on yet another project. This time it was a film called *Rounders* by John Dahl about the world of illegal gambling, which began shooting in New York in December 1997. Although *Rounders* did not have the artistic flair of Coppola's work or the large budget of a Spielberg film, Damon believed it had a message to contribute to the film industry. "The movie is about following the road less traveled," Damon explained. "I can definitely relate to that as an actor. Dropping out of college and coming to Hollywood to try to make it in the movies is not the brightest idea in the world. It's something you're compelled to do."[78]

In *Rounders* Damon plays former gambler Mike McDermott, who leaves his girlfriend and law school after being lured back into illegal poker by his friend Worm (played by Edward Norton), who has just been released from prison. Worm owes a huge gambling debt to a Russian mobster (played by John Malkovich), and when McDermott steps in to vouch for Worm he finds himself a target of the mobster's wrath. McDermott hits the illegal poker circuit to make the $15,000 to pay Worm's debt within two days. In the process he realizes he never really wanted the straight life or law school. He embraces professional gambling and regains his passion for life.

In his usual way, Damon prepared for the role of McDermott by immersing himself in his character's world. Before shooting began, he and his costar Edward Norton attended private, legal underground poker games in New York to get a feel for the gambling world and learn how serious poker

Although the film Rounders *received much criticism, Damon believes in the film's artistic value.*

players behave. Damon found himself studying the "art" of making a poker face and the body language and strategies that poker players use to identify easy victims.

Despite Damon's belief in the film, *Rounders* did only modestly well at the box office when it was released in late summer 1998. Although highly publicized, with Damon's now-recognized name topping the cast, by October the film had earned less than $20 million, small by most industry standards. Some critics blamed the film for its failure to make illegal poker and all its accompanying jargon (such as "pushka" and "belly buster") relative to the average person, and many accused it of idealizing illegal gambling. Damon, however, dismisses the charge that *Rounders* romanticizes the world of gambling, pointing out that the movie only uses poker as a medium to tell a story about the choices people make in their lives.

Critics also thought that Damon's McDermott character lacked a believable motivation for his gambling obsession. *New York Times* film critic Janet Maslin said, "[The] film has character in oversupply even if its actual characters are sometimes thin. Poker fever makes up for whatever the story lacks in everyday emotions."[79] However, Damon's acting itself was praised, and the film, though small, did keep him in the public eye coming on the heels of his Academy Award and *Saving Private Ryan.*

Dogma

While Damon was still working on the set of *Rounders,* his old friend Kevin Smith offered him a role in his comedy *Dogma* (1999). Damon jumped at the chance to work with Smith and his best friend Affleck, who had also been offered a part in the film. *Dogma* was to be a religious satire costarring comedian Chris Rock, British actor Alan Rickman, Linda Fiorentino, and Joey Lauren Adams (Affleck's costar in Smith's *Chasing Amy*). Damon decided to do *Dogma* because it was a change of pace from serious drama to comic relief, and also because he was impressed with the intelligent humor in the script.

Ironically, from the time of its premiere in the fall of 1999, the public attention paid to *Dogma* was anything but comic relief. The film's content was the subject of much public consternation. In the movie, Damon and Affleck play a pair of fallen angels who are plotting a way to return to heaven after being banished forever to the state of Wisconsin. When *Dogma* was shown as part of the respected New York Film Festival, protesters stood outside the Lincoln Center for the Performing Arts singing and praying for the demise of what they considered a sacrilegious film. One of the protesters, Bev Santini of Garden City, New York, explained, "We are here to tell people that we're looking for more respect and love, and less criticizing of each other's faith. We're praying for [the filmmakers] so that they stop ridiculing Christians . . . in the world."[80]

Contrary to the protesters' view, Miramax, which released the film, director Kevin Smith, and Matt Damon all stood behind their movie, emphasizing that *Dogma* does not ridicule religion but strives to put it in a lighter context. Critics also praised the film, including *New York Times*'s Janet Maslin, who wrote, "Yes, Mr. Smith enjoys shock value, but this time he makes it mercilessly funny and places it in the context of an obviously devout, enlightened parable [a moral story]."[81]

In the film Dogma, *Damon and Aflleck play fallen angels scheming a way back into heaven.*

The public controversy surrounding *Dogma* aroused curiosity in moviegoers. Although not a box office smash, *Dogma* became enormously popular and did quite well. Despite the fact that neither of his last two films had enjoyed the success that *Good Will Hunting* had, Damon was not concerned. Since 1997 when he began working on *The Rainmaker,* he had been constantly working.

Not only were offers coming, but big paychecks were now attached to some of them. Damon, however, has never been one to choose his roles based on money. Although he now commands about $5 million per movie, he is not above taking substantially less if he thinks the role is a good one. For instance, Damon was quite content with the $600,000 he made for *Rounders.*

The Talented Mr. Ripley

However, Damon had no problems accepting the lead role—and the large paycheck—in 1999 when Anthony Minghella (of the 1996 Oscar-winning *The English Patient*) offered him the part of Tom Ripley, a charming but deadly sociopath. The role of Ripley would give Damon yet another opportunity to expand his acting skills, and to play a part completely different from any he had done previously. "It's certainly the most unconventional in terms of movies I've done. . . . The guy [Ripley] goes and falls in love with this man [the character Dickie Greenleaf] and his life—to the point where he wants to be in his skin." [82]

Minghella's movie, titled *The Talented Mr. Ripley,* is based on a 1956 novel by Patricia Highsmith, and chronicles the growing web of deception and murder constructed by Ripley. In the movie, Ripley is overwhelmed with desire for his friend Dickie Greenleaf's rich and luxurious lifestyle. Eventually Ripley murders Greenleaf (played by British actor Jude Law) and assumes his identity, but in his effort to preserve his secret he commits murder after murder. The only person who suspects him is Greenleaf's girlfriend, Marge (played by Gwyneth Paltrow), who barely escapes Ripley's deadly intentions near the end.

When the film premiered on December 25, 1999, audiences were dumbfounded by Damon's performance. Critics praised his ability to portray a murderous sociopath as a vulnerable person. Damon explained how he used his character's underlying emotions to connect with the audience:

> I think he [Ripley] does despicable things, but the whole challenge of the movie was to keep the audience with

Arguably Damon's most challenging role, The Talented Mr. Ripley *proved Damon's versatility as an actor.*

Ripley. Not that they're sympathetic, but that they understand. You know, they disagree with what he does but they understand because they know where it's coming from. It's this deep loneliness that this guy has . . . and he's so desperately trying not to be alone throughout the rest of the movie.[83]

Media predictions that Damon's portrayal of a psychopath would damage his career proved groundless, as critics and audiences praised his work in the film. *The Talented Mr. Ripley* not only performed well at the box office but it earned Damon his second Golden Globe nomination for Best Actor.

The Legend of Bagger Vance

Damon's next big film project was *The Legend of Bagger Vance*, which gave him the opportunity to work with director Robert Redford, another director he had always admired. Damon was also attracted to the film's theme—losing one's direction or purpose in life— which was paralleled in the story by the golfer losing his swing.

In *The Legend of Bagger Vance,* Damon plays the golfer, a World War I veteran named Rannulf Junuh who has lost his direction in life when he meets up with a mysterious caddy named Bagger Vance (played by Will Smith). Damon explains what caused his character's inner turmoil: "Junuh's problem was that through the war he came in contact with a world where there are no rules. Suddenly life makes no sense. It turns upside down. He disengages [emotionally] and loses his soul."[84] Bagger Vance encourages Junuh to return to the sport of his prewar days—golf. He shows the reluctant Junuh many tricks to winning the game, including how to get his excellent golf swing back. In the process he regains a sense of purpose—and the love of his life (played by Charlize Theron).

As usual, Damon prepared for the role of Junuh with vigor. He had never played golf before and had to learn how to swing—and he was determined to learn to swing like the best. Unfortunately for Damon, one day he swung down with such force that the club hit the ground at an odd angle and twisted Damon's torso, causing him to separate a rib. Damon was not about to let this prevent him from performing, so Redford hired a chiropractor to be on the set

In The Legend of Bagger Vance, *Damon, pictured here with Will Smith, plays a World War I veteran named Rannulf Junuh.*

to realign Damon's rib whenever necessary. "It hurt every subsequent swing because I would dislocate the rib all over again," explained Damon. "It turned into a routine. I'd step up to the tee and Tony the chiro would stand up just off the camera. I'd swing and act as if I was not in pain. Robert Redford would yell 'cut.' I'd wince and Tony would run over and pop my rib back in."[85]

Despite Damon's belief in the film and his physical sacrifice for the role, when *The Legend of Bagger Vance* was released on November 3, 2000, critics almost universally expressed disappointment in the film. While acknowledging the talent of the actors and the director involved, they complained that the film lacked intelligent dialogue and that the characters failed to evoke much sympathy from viewers. "Redford is so fascinated with the mythical qualities of the novel's premise . . . he doesn't realize how [emotionally flat] the tale really is," said the *Miami Herald*. "Damon and Theron do what they can with their thinly written characters and emerge unscathed."[86]

Despite the criticism, the film brought in $12 million its opening weekend, placing third among all the movies in theaters at the time. Damon believes the charm of this modern "fairy tale" will win audiences over with its message—that everyone has something they are good at that makes life worth living.

All the Pretty Horses

Damon's next project was *All the Pretty Horses,* directed by Billy Bob Thornton. Like *The Legend of Bagger Vance,* the film focuses on the purpose of living. Damon enjoys scripts with moral lessons and was attracted to the character because of the challenge of portraying a young person who undergoes personal trials in the quest for maturity.

The film, based on the book by Cormac McCarthy, tells the story of Texas teenager John Grady Cole (played by Damon), who rides off to Mexico in search of adventure after his mother sells the family ranch. During the trip, he and his friend Lacey Rawlins (played by Henry Thomas) pick up a thirteen-year-old misfit named Blevins (played by Lucas Black). The three young men eventually find work breaking horses at a hacienda, where Grady falls in love with the ranch owner's beautiful daughter, Alejandra (played by Penelope Cruz). However, the romance lands Grady in

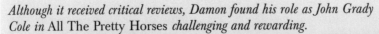

Although it received critical reviews, Damon found his role as John Grady Cole in All The Pretty Horses *challenging and rewarding.*

a Mexican jail, where he is involved in a murder committed in self-defense. Suddenly the adventurous youth is forced to look deep inside himself to find the principles that will give him the strength to endure.

Despite the moral intensity of the film, when *All the Pretty Horses* was released on December 25, 2000, the critical reception was mixed. *Entertainment Weekly* found fault with the film, saying, "Damon . . . generating his all weather expression of earnestness, does not look at ease anywhere near either wild horses or wild women . . . but most of it is the fault of . . . [the] direction: perhaps Thornton didn't know what he wanted from scene to scene and where he wanted to arrive at in the end." [87] Many critics thought the theme of the movie got lost in the artsy filming and flat dialogue.

However, some critics appreciated the artsy quality of *All the Pretty Horses,* though acknowledging that it might not appeal to large audiences. Chicago film critic Michael Wilmington wrote, "though it may wind up perplexing as many audiences as it moves or delights, this . . . passionately respectful adaptation of McCarthy's saga ranks as a major achievement of the last movie year. . . . The acting is exemplary. Damon and Thomas . . . bring their characters alive and Damon gives the movie a calm, shining center." [88]

Public reception to *All the Pretty Horses* has been modest. However, commercial success has never been the top priority for Damon, and he continues to stand by his choice of films. He considers the film a piece of art rather than entertainment.

Current Projects

In addition to his continuous film projects, Damon is finding other mediums for expressing his creativity. Most of these projects allow him to perform work other than acting, such as producing and script writing.

Currently he and Ben Affleck are producing a new reality-based television show called *The Runner.* The show is scheduled to be aired live by ABC during the summer of 2001. The purpose of the show is to follow a person selected to be "the runner" who must escape capture in the continental United States for thirty days. The runner must perform specific tasks, such as visiting a McDonald's in Arizona during a set twenty-four-hour period of time or taking a tour of a Coors Brewery in Golden, Colorado, within a forty-eight-hour block of time. If the runner performs the tasks without being captured, at the end of the thirty days he or she wins a million dollars. Television viewers can follow the runner by watching the show and checking in on a website that tracks the contestant. Viewers can help pinpoint the runner's location and participate in the capture. If a viewer captures the runner, the viewer wins the million dollars instead. Andrea Wong, ABC's vice president of alternative series and specials, believes that Damon and Affleck's show will be a success. "The thing I love about Runner is that anyone in America can be involved in the show whenever they want to be," she explained. "It is a huge initiative for the network. We think it's going to be a huge event, and we're putting a huge amount of resources into it."[89]

Damon and Affleck are also doing something to make the road to success for new screenwriters easier than it was for them. Through their new media entertainment company LivePlanet, they launched a project called Greenlight that offers an online script-writing contest. Only aspiring screenwriters, not professionals, may submit their scripts to the Greenlight website. The twist is that all the contestants must then read and review three other submitted scripts and come to a decision as to the winner. Damon and Affleck will produce the winning screenplay with Miramax on a budget of about $1 million. In addition, the making of the film will air on HBO as a thirteen-episode series in the fall of 2001.

Damon, who still enjoys storytelling, and Affleck continue to do screen writing of their own. They are currently working on a script for Castle Rock, a stipulation that was made when Castle Rock allowed them to put the script of *Good Will Hunting* in turnaround. During 1999 and 2000, they found scraps of time to work on the screenplay called *Halfway House*, which is about counselors working in a mental rehabilitation institution. Like they did with *Good Will Hunting*, the pair based the story on what they knew to be true, this time the stories told to them by a friend who worked in such an institution. In it Affleck will play a counselor and Damon will play one of the mentally ill patients. True to their longtime support of each other's careers, Damon's role will be supporting this time, while Affleck's will be the leading part. The film is scheduled to hit theaters in 2001, but currently there is no specific release date.

Surviving the Fanfare

Throughout his acting career, Matt Damon has always said he wanted success for only two reasons: one, to gain respect for his work, and two, to give him the freedom and power to control his career. Having this respect and power is an important part of how Damon is now able to secure professionally challenging roles and intelligent scripts with respected directors.

The fame itself is not what Damon values. Around 1998, when asked how he felt about his new status as a Hollywood star, Damon humbly replied,

> I like it. I don't think I'm addicted to what is involved with it. I really could take it or leave it. So far, I'd have to say I don't quite know what you're talking about. Honestly. I haven't met a single person, I have not walked down the street where somebody stopped me and said, 'Oh, you're

Despite the professional success that Damon has achieved so early in life, he doesn't allow the fame to go to his head.

Matt Damon.' . . . Which is normal since not that many people know my work, and which works fine for me: I want to be in a position where I can go wherever the character I'm researching is supposed to be from. . . . The nice thing is I'm in a position now where they're actually paying for me to do it. I mean, they're putting me [up] during the time when I research, which I used to have to [pay] out of pocket.[90]

So far Damon has resisted developing a big ego and seems to guard himself from letting fame go to his head. He credits his mother, Nancy Carlsson-Paige, with instilling this self-discipline in him, and he frequently says that if he ever did become affected by fame, his family would be the first to reel him in and slap some sense into him. As Damon explains, "My family doesn't let me get away with anything. They bring me back down to earth and make me realize that my fame doesn't absolve me of being a good human being."[91]

However, there seem to be a lot of people acquainted with Matt Damon who believe that if anybody can beat the downfalls of fame and fortune, he can. Miramax's Harvey Weinstein described Damon as "exceptionally bright, honest, and level-headed and has both feet planted firmly on the ground, which is a hard thing to do in this business."[92] Brian Dennehy, who worked with Damon on *Rising Son* in 1990, cited Damon's extreme sense of self-discipline as the key to his dedication, hard work, and focus in his career. Francis Ford Coppola, who directed Damon in *The Rainmaker*, sums up why Matt Damon has a better than most chance at maintaining his Hollywood success:

Actors like Matt are in as good a position as they've ever been. They've become the trademarks of the movies, not the directors. There's barely a movie that can be made without [Nicolas] Cage or [Harrison] Ford or [Brad] Pitt. Now they determine what movies get made. Matt has got the gift—and he's a writer in his own right. That gives him something special.[93]

Notes

Introduction: The Quest for Perfection

1. Quoted in Chris Nickson, *Matt Damon: An Unauthorized Biography*. Los Angeles: Renaissance Books, 1999, p. 102.
2. Quoted in Elizabeth A. Schick, ed., *Current Biography Yearbook*. New York: H. W. Wilson, 1998, p. 7.

Chapter 1: An Influential Childhood

3. Quoted in Maxine Diamond and Harriet Hemmings, *Matt Damon: A Biography*. New York: Pocket Books, 1998, p. 4.
4. Quoted in Nickson, *Matt Damon*, pp. 18–19.
5. Quoted in Nickson, *Matt Damon*, p. 20.
6. Quoted in Nickson, *Matt Damon*, p. 19.
7. Quoted in Nickson, *Matt Damon*, p. 21.
8. Quoted in Nickson, *Matt Damon*, p. 21.
9. Quoted in Belinda Luscombe, "Matt Damon Acts Out," *Time*, December 27, 1999, p. 2.
10. Quoted in Diamond and Hemmings, *Matt Damon*, p. 6.
11. Quoted in Luscombe, "Matt Damon Acts Out," p.1.
12. Quoted in Diamond and Hemmings, *Matt Damon*, p. 6.
13. Quoted in Diamond and Hemmings, *Matt Damon*, pp. 6–7.
14. Quoted in the Official Matt Damon Website, www.mattdamon.com/profile/quotes/index.html.
15. Quoted in the Official Matt Damon Website, www.mattdamon.com/profile/bio/2.html.
16. Quoted in Nickson, *Matt Damon*, p. 26.
17. Quoted in Diamond and Hemmings, *Matt Damon*, p. 11.

18. Quoted in Nickson, *Matt Damon*, p. 27.
19. Quoted in Diamond and Hemmings, *Matt Damon*, p. 13.
20. Quoted in Nickson, *Matt Damon*, p. 30.
21. Quoted in Diamond and Hemmings, *Matt Damon*, p. 11.
22. Quoted in Nickson, *Matt Damon*, p. 29.
23. Quoted in Nickson, *Matt Damon*, p. 31.
24. Quoted in Diamond and Hemmings, *Matt Damon*, p. 15.

Chapter 2: The Harvard Years

25. Quoted in Nickson, *Matt Damon*, p. 37.
26. Quoted in "Mr. Nice Guy: Is the Star of *Good Will Hunting* Too Good to Be True?" Platform Online interview, December 1997, www.platform.net/fuel/12_97/03matt/interview.html.
27. Quoted in Diamond and Hemmings, *Matt Damon*, p. 16.
28. Quoted in Diamond and Hemmings, *Matt Damon*, p. 17.
29. Quoted in Nickson, *Matt Damon*, p. 45.
30. Quoted in Nickson, *Matt Damon*, p. 46.
31. Quoted in Diamond and Hemmings, *Matt Damon*, p. 27.
32. Quoted in Nickson, *Matt Damon*, p. 57.
33. Quoted in Nickson, *Matt Damon*, p. 56.
34. Quoted in Nickson, *Matt Damon*, p. 59.
35. Quoted in Nickson, *Matt Damon*, p. 65.

Chapter 3: A Dash of Good Will

36. Quoted in Nickson, *Matt Damon*, p. 68.
37. Quoted in Nickson, *Matt Damon*, p. 73.
38. Quoted in Diamond and Hemmings, *Matt Damon*, p. 21.
39. Quoted in Nickson, *Matt Damon*, p. 63.
40. Quoted in Nickson, *Matt Damon*, p. 73.
41. Quoted in Nickson, *Matt Damon*, p. 73.
42. Quoted in Nickson, *Matt Damon*, p. 74.
43. Quoted in Diamond and Hemmings, *Matt Damon*, p. 33.
44. Quoted in Schick, *Current Biography Yearbook*, p. 4.
45. Quoted in Nickson, *Matt Damon*, pp. 86–87.
46. Quoted in Nickson, *Matt Damon*, p. 88.
47. Quoted in Nickson, *Matt Damon*, p. 89.
48. Quoted in Nickson, *Matt Damon*, p. 90.

Chapter 4: The Breakthrough

49. Quoted in Diamond and Hemmings, *Matt Damon*, p. 23.
50. Quoted in Nickson, *Matt Damon*, p. 98.
51. Quoted in Nickson, *Matt Damon*, p. 99.
52. Quoted in Nickson, *Matt Damon*, p. 102.
53. Quoted in Nickson, *Matt Damon*, p. 92.
54. Platform Online interview.
55. Quoted in Nickson, *Matt Damon*, p. 114.
56. Quoted in Nickson, *Matt Damon*, p. 115.
57. Quoted in Nickson, *Matt Damon*, p. 116.
58. Quoted in Nickson, *Matt Damon*, pp. 136–37.
59. Quoted in Nickson, *Matt Damon*, p. 119.
60. Quoted in Schick, *Current Biography Yearbook*, p. 6.

Chapter 5: The Making of a Star

61. Quoted in Nickson, *Matt Damon*, p. 139.
62. Quoted in Nickson, *Matt Damon*, p. 142.
63. Quoted in Laura Smith Kay, "Matt Damon: Making It Good," People Online, www.people.aol.com/people/sp/damon/damon 2.html.
64. Quoted in Kay, "Matt Damon: Making It Good."
65. Quoted in David Blum, "Reign Man," *Time*, December 1, 1997, p. 79.
66. Janet Maslin, *"John Grisham's The Rainmaker"* (review), *New York Times*, November 21, 1997.
67. Janet Maslin, *"Good Will Hunting"* (review), *New York Times*, December 5, 1997.
68. Quoted in Nickson, *Matt Damon*, p. 157.
69. Quoted in Nickson, *Matt Damon*, p. 158.
70. Quoted in Nickson, *Matt Damon*, p. 160.
71. Quoted in Nickson, *Matt Damon*, p. 166.
72. Quoted in Diamond and Hemmings, *Matt Damon*, p. 49.
73. Quoted in Nickson, *Matt Damon*, p. 173.
74. Quoted in Blum, "Reign Man," p. 79.

Chapter 6: Hollywood Golden Boy

75. Quoted in Nickson, *Matt Damon*, p. 142.

76. Quoted in Schick, *Current Biography Yearbook*, p. 7.

77. Quoted in Nickson, *Matt Damon*, p. 176.

78. Quoted in Nickson, *Matt Damon*, p. 181.

79. Janet Maslin, "*Rounders:* Knowing When to Hold 'em and Fold 'em but Just Not When to Run" (review), *New York Times*, September 11, 1998.

80. Quoted in "Dogma Draws Protests," Mr. Showbiz News, October 5, 1999, www.mrshowbiz.go.com.

81. Quoted in "Dogma Draws Protests."

82. Quoted in Diamond and Hemmings, *Matt Damon*, p. 55.

83. Quoted in Eric Floren, "The Talented Matt Damon," Toronto Jam Website, www.fortunecity.com/lavendar/fullmonty/282/JamRipley.htm.

84. Quoted in Louis B. Hobson, "Game Boy," *Calgary Sun*, November 2, 2000.

85. Quoted in Hobson, "Game Boy."

86. Rene Rodriguez, "*The Legend of Bagger Vance*" (review), *Miami Herald*, November 3, 2000.

87. Lisa Schwarzbaum, "*All the Pretty Horses*" (review), *Entertainment Weekly*, December 22, 2000.

88. Michael Wilmington, "*All the Pretty Horses*" (review), Metromix Chicago Movies, www.zap2it.com/custom/components/metromix2/contentarticle/0,2176,4401,00.html.

89. "What Do These Guys Know About the Internet?" *Fortune*, October 9, 2000, p. 112.

90. "Matt Damon on Life in the Limelight," www.damon.8m.com/fameq.htm.

91. Quoted in Diamond and Hemmings, *Matt Damon*, p. 64.

92. Quoted in Diamond and Hemmings, *Matt Damon*, p. 66.

93. Quoted in Blum, "Reign Man," p.80.

Important Dates in the Life of Matt Damon

1970

Matthew Paige Damon is born in Boston, Massachusetts, on October 8.

1972

Damon's parents get a divorce.

1980

Damon's mother moves him and his brother, Kyle, to a communal house in Cambridge, Massachusetts; Damon meets and befriends eight-year-old Ben Affleck.

1988

Damon makes his film debut in *Mystic Pizza;* he enters Harvard University as a freshman.

1990

Damon appears in his first significant role in the cable television movie *Rising Son.*

1992

Damon appears in *School Ties;* he drops out of Harvard to move to California and pursue acting full-time.

1993

Damon appears in *Geronimo: An American Legend;* Damon and Affleck work on the script of *Good Will Hunting.*

1994

Damon and Affleck sell the script of *Good Will Hunting* to Castle Rock Entertainment for $600,000.

1995

Castle Rock puts the script of *Good Will Hunting* into turn-around, and Miramax buys it for nearly $1 million.

1996

Damon appears in *Courage Under Fire.*

1997

Damon appears in his first lead role in John Grisham's *The Rainmaker;* he stars in *Good Will Hunting.*

1998

Damon appears in the title role in *Saving Private Ryan;* he stars in *Rounders;* Damon and Affleck win the Golden Globe Award for Best Screenplay and the Academy Award for Best Original Screenplay for *Good Will Hunting.*

1999

Damon appears in *Dogma* and *The Talented Mr. Ripley* for which he earns a Golden Globe nomination for his acting.

2000

Damon appears in *The Legend of Bagger Vance* and *All the Pretty Horses.*

For Further Reading

Books

Mark Bego, *Matt Damon: Chasing a Dream*. Kansas City, MO: Andrews McMeel, 1998. This book offers an in-depth look at the driving forces in Damon's life—his friendship with Ben Affleck, his family, and his desire to be the best at what he does.

Brian J. Robb, *The Matt Damon Album: The Making of a Star*. London: Plexus, 2000. This biography focuses on Damon's friendship with Ben Affleck and his numerous film roles. It includes fifty photos.

Kathleen Tracy, *Matt Damon*. New York: St. Martin's Paperbacks, 1998. An overview of Damon's life that includes eight pages of photos.

Periodicals

Rebecca Ascher-Walsh, "Ben Affleck and Matt Damon," *Entertainment Weekly*, February 13, 1998. This article includes information on many of Damon's awards and his performance in *Good Will Hunting*.

Anne Christensen, "Meet Matt Damon," *Vanity Fair*, December 1997. Written during the premiere of both *The Rainmaker* and *Good Will Hunting*, this article offers a brief overview of Damon's life.

Justine Elias, "Matt Damon," *US*, February 1998. An exclusive interview with Damon.

"Matt Damon," *Drama-Logue*, November 20–26, 1997. A brief overview of Damon's life and work.

Jerry Roberts, "Peers Recall Damon's Good Will," *Variety*, March 12, 1998. This article includes stories shared by childhood friends who remembered Damon in his youth.

Websites

Good Matt Damon (www.goodmattdamon.com).This comprehen-
    sive website provides a long biography, nearly twenty magazine
    articles on Damon, news updates, a photo gallery, and a list of
    Damon's awards. This site also conducts weekly polls on chang-
    ing topics, such as "What is your favorite Matt Damon film?"
Official Matt Damon Website (www.mattdamon.com). This site in-
    cludes a quote section, filmography, a list of Damon's awards, a
    biography, and news updates.

Works Consulted

Books

Maxine Diamond and Harriet Hemmings, *Matt Damon: A Biography.* New York: Pocket Books, 1998. This book offers an overview of Damon's life and work, including sections on his romances, his horoscope (he is a Libra), the top ten Matt Damon websites, and trivia about Damon.

Chris Nickson, *Matt Damon: An Unauthorized Biography.* Los Angeles: Renaissance Books, 1999. This biography provides an in-depth look at the forces that have shaped Damon's life and career, including his unorthodox childhood and his intense dedication to professional perfection. It also includes a detailed filmography and a section on Matt Damon websites.

Elizabeth A. Schick, ed., *Current Biography Yearbook.* New York: H. W. Wilson, 1998. This brief entry covers the lives and burgeoning careers of both Damon and Affleck. It includes many quotes from interviews and periodicals.

Periodicals

David Blum, "Reign Man," *Time,* December 1, 1997. This article offers a close look at Damon on the cusp of success just as *The Rainmaker* and *Good Will Hunting* premiered. It includes summaries of his films through 1997 and discusses Damon's skepticism about fame.

"Ciao, Romance: The It Couple Becomes a Split Couple," *People Weekly,* May 8, 2000. An overview of Damon's relationship with Winona Ryder and speculation about their breakup.

Louis B. Hobson, "Game Boy," *Calgary Sun*, November 2, 2000. This newspaper article discusses Damon's motivations for making *The Legend of Bagger Vance* and includes comments by Damon on the subject of fame.

"Hunks Show Good Will to Janitors," *Boston Herald*, May 7, 2000. Discusses Damon and Affleck's participation in a Harvard rally to raise wages for school janitors.

Belinda Luscombe, "Matt Damon Acts Out," *Time*, December 27, 1999. This exclusive article includes in-depth information about Damon's childhood, his family, and his experiences making *The Talented Mr. Ripley.*

Nick Madigan, "Bad Vibes Haunt *Good Will* Oscar Nomination," *Variety*, March 16, 1998. This brief article prior to the 1998 Academy Awards examines the allegations made regarding the origin of the *Good Will Hunting* script.

Janet Maslin, "*Good Will Hunting*" (review), *New York Times*, December 5, 1997. Maslin offers an exceptional review of this film along with a summary of it.

———, "*John Grisham's The Rainmaker*" (review), *New York Times*, November 21, 1997. This review of Damon's breakout film provides a positive analysis of his performance as well as a summary.

———, "*Rounders:* Knowing When to Hold 'em and Fold 'em but Just Not When to Run" (review), *New York Times*, September 11, 1998. This review provides both positive and negative aspects of the film and includes a film summary.

John Nichols, "Unfair Harvard," *Nation,* June 5, 2000. This brief article includes quotes and details from Damon and Affleck's participation in the Harvard janitor rally.

Rene Rodriguez, "*The Legend of Bagger Vance*" (review), *Miami Herald,* November 3, 2000. This newspaper review presents many of the negative aspects of the film but praises Damon's talents.

Lisa Schwarzbaum, "*All the Pretty Horses*" (review), *Entertainment Weekly*, December 22, 2000. This review of the movie provides scathing criticism of its dialogue, lack of rapport between the cast members, and its "high art" presentation, which places much of its meaning out of reach of many audiences.

Bob Strauss, "Anything Goes . . . for the Talented Mr. Damon," *L.A. Daily News*, January 3, 2000. This newspaper article offers exclusive information about Damon's experience filming *The Talented Mr. Ripley*, including an analysis of the Ripley character.

"What Do These Guys Know About Internet?" *Fortune*, October 9, 2000. This long article includes information about Damon and Affleck's current ventures, including their new media company LivePlanet, their script-writing contest (Project Greenlight), and their reality-based television show, *The Runner*.

Internet Sources

"Dogma Draws Protests," Mr. Showbiz News, October 5, 1999. www.mrshowbiz.go.com. Analyzes the public controversy over the film's religious satire.

Eric Floren, "The Talented Matt Damon," Toronto Jam Website. www.fortunecity.com/lavendar/fullmonty/282/JamRipley.htm. This article analyzes Damon's portrayal of Tom Ripley and includes an account of his "audition" with Anthony Minghella.

Laura Smith Kay, "Matt Damon: Making It Good," People Online.www.people.aol.com/people/sp/damon/damon2.html. This long article offers an overview of Damon and Affleck's friendship, Damon's film roles through 1997, and comments about Damon's abilities by directors Anthony Minghella and Gus Van Sant. It also scrutinizes *Good Will Hunting*'s chances of winning Oscar status prior to the ceremony.

"Matt Damon on Life in the Limelight," www.damon.8m.com/fameq.htm. This page provides a wealth of Damon quotes on various topics.

"Mr. Nice Guy: Is the Star of *Good Will Hunting* Too Good to Be True?" Platform Online interview. www.platform.net/fuel/12_97/03matt/interview.html. In this 1997 interview Damon discusses his newly acquired fame, his Harvard education, his opinion about the Hollywood film industry, his friendship with Affleck, and his plans for the future. He also talks about writing and making the film *Good Will Hunting*.

Michael Wilmington, "*All the Pretty Horses*" (review), Metromix Chicago Movies. www.zap2it.com/custom/components/ metromix2/contentarticle/0,2176,4401,00.html. A positive review of the film, summarizing the story line and explaining the moral parallels presented through the artsy quality of the movie.

Index

Picture Credits

Cover photo: The Liaison Agency Network/Alain Benainous
Archive/Reuters/Sam Mircovich, 60
Archive/Reuters/Claudio Papi, 15
Archive/Reuters/Fred Prouser, 9
Archive/Reuters/Blakse Sell, 77
Classmates.com Yearbook Archives, 20, 23, 24
Corbis/Kevin Fleming, 17
Corbis/Bill Ross, 30
Photofest, 10, 33, 35, 37, 41, 43, 44, 46, 52, 54, 55, 57, 64, 67, 68,
    69, 71, 73, 80, 84, 86, 87, 89, 90, 93
Photofest/Phillip Caruso, 63
Photofest/David James, 81
Photofest/George Kraychyk, 61, 74
Photofest/Ralph Nelson, 49

About the Author

Christina M. Girod received her undergraduate degree from the University of California at Santa Barbara. She worked with speech- and language-impaired students and taught elementary school for six years in Denver, Colorado. She has written scores of short biographies as well as organizational and country profiles for educational multimedia materials. The topics she has covered include both historical and current sketches of politicians, humanitarians, environmentalists, and entertainers. She has also written *Native Americans of the Southeast* (Indigenous Peoples of North America series) and *Down Syndrome* and *Learning Disabilities* (both Diseases and Disorders series) for Lucent Books. Girod lives in Santa Maria, California, with her husband, Jon Pierre, and daughter, Joni.